Katherine Dunlap Cather

Boyhood Stories of Famous Men

CLASSIC PAGES

Dunlap Cather, Katherine

Boyhood Stories of Famous Men

ISBN/EAN: 978-3-86741-428-9

First published in 2010 by Europaeischer Hochschulverlag GmbH & Co KG, Bremen, Germany.

© Europaeischer Hochschulverlag GmbH & Co KG, Fahrenheitstr. 1, D-28359 Bremen (www.ehv-online.com). All rights reserved.

This book is a reproduction of an out of print title and has originally been published by The Century (New York) in 1917. Because no electronic master copies of this title could be obtained, the publisher had to reuse old copies of the text. We therefore apologize for any possible loss in quality.

BOYHOOD STORIES OF FAMOUS MEN

TITIAN ❦ CHOPIN ❦ ANDRE DEL SARTO
THORWALDSEN ❦ MENDELSSOHN ❦ MOZART
MURILLO ❦ STRADIVARIUS ❦ GUIDO RENI
CLAUDE LORRAINE ❦ TINTORETTO
& ROSA BONHEUR "TOMBOY OF BORDEAUX"

BY
KATHERINE DUNLAP CATHER

ILLUSTRATED
BY M. L. BOWER

NEW YORK
THE CENTURY CO.
1917

To
MY MOTHER

HOW IT HAPPENED

Once upon a time there was a little girl who journeyed very often into an enchanted valley. In it were rainbow-colored meadows, marvelous fruits and flowers and singing birds, and forests such as never grew in any country out of dreamland. Fairies and gnomes and sprites danced there by night, and along the crystal rivers of that land Merlin wrought his wizardry, bringing King Arthur and all his noble knights back to life again. There Sindbad the Sailor walked side by side with Robin Hood; there Aladdin carried his wonder lamp past the balcony where Juliet waited for Romeo; and there the children of Hamelin town, following the piper to the mountain gate, smiled at grave-eyed Carl making pictures by the Stove of Nuremberg. Richard Cœur de Lion and the crusaders rode over its shining highways as they moved toward Palestine, and several times Puck broke right through the procession, whereupon the Lion Heart had to remarshal his forces before they could go on. The whole great company of story folk gathered there, and the only way mortals could enter was to become acquainted with some member of the enchanted company who could lead them in. Thus, through the books she read and the tales she heard, the little girl came to know many a hero at whose beckoning the gates swung open, and she beheld the glories beyond them.

But after a while she took no more journeys into the valley, for although she met many splendid book people, not one of them had the power to take her back. Instead of walking under spreading trees with the enchanted company, she had to stay in the world without, and live in the memory of beautiful days spent beyond the magic gates. Always, however, things seem to come out right, after all, for one morning between the covers of a dingy book, she found just what she had been seeking. In "The Child of Urbino," Ouida's lovely tribute to the great Raphael, was one who could take her into the rainbow country. The gates swung wide, and she went in again with the painter.

HOW IT HAPPENED

Years afterward, when she was grown, she still remembered and loved "The Child of Urbino," partly because of its beauty, partly because of all it had meant to her. It had shown her the way into a wonderful realm. It had caused her to realize that the stories of great creators are just as fascinating as those of Ali Baba, Sigurd the Volsung, the troubadours who sang in Provence, or the crusaders who fought in Palestine, and that by knowing them and their works the gates of the enchanted valley would never close to her. It taught her to look for the stories underlying great pictures and melodies; and, having found many, the thought occurred to her that she ought to share her treasures with boys and girls who would enjoy them.

So one day, under the magnolias of a California garden, she went to work, and out of that morning's record grew the story, "The Whittler of Cremona." A kindly editor liked it and asked for another, and thus "Boyhood Stories of Famous Men" came to be.

The facts that make up the tales have been

gathered through many years and in many places, some from libraries in great American cities and universities, some from dusty manuscripts in museums and private collections across the sea, some from the lips of peasants who repeated legends handed down from the olden time. Most of them have already appeared in the St. Nicholas magazine; and now, through the pages of the book they come to you. May they lead you into the fascinating world of melody and color; may they open the magic gates for you just as that other story once opened them for me, into that rainbow country where delights are never ending.

KATHERINE DUNLAP CATHER.

TABLE OF CONTENTS

CHAPTER		PAGE
I	THE BOY OF CADORE	3
II	WHEN MOZART RACED WITH MARIE ANTOINETTE	23
III	THE TOMBOY FROM BORDEAUX	43
IV	JACOPO, THE LITTLE DYER	65
V	BARTOLOME'S VELVET HAT	85
VI	THE WHITTLER OF CREMONA	101
VII	A BIT O' PINK VERBENA	117
VIII	A SHEPHERD LAD OF TUSCANY	139
IX	THE BORDER WONDERFUL	159
X	THE WONDER-CHILD OF WARSAW	175
XI	THE LIGHT OF GUIDO'S LAMP	197
XII	OLD JAN'S TWILIGHT TALE	223
XIII	WHEN THE PRINCESS PASSED	241
XIV	THE JOYOUS VAGABOND	259

LIST OF ILLUSTRATIONS

PAGE

Some day he would bring honor to his name
and glory to Poland . . . . *Frontispiece*

They had spent the afternoon blossom hunting . . 5

A group of folk moved toward the building where
the lad waited 16

Away they went, Marie's yellow curls flying . . . 26

Wolfgang thought only of the music 35

The grandfather stood by the stone gate calling good-
by as they drove away 45

The room that was her workshop came to be a sort
of Noah's Ark 56

Jacopo began his work with the Master 73

Whenever he passed a gaudily skirted market-girl, he
saluted with the air of a grandee 87

Memories of the moor 93

Day after day he toiled in the workshop 107

Then Giotto went to the city 150

"Upon the word of an honest Florentine it *is* the
work of a lad" 167

He scarcely breathed, for Catalani was singing . . . 189

"And you, Bertel Thorwaldsen, what do you want?" . 227

Wonderful, roseate days began 273

THE BOY OF CADORE

BOYHOOD STORIES OF FAMOUS MEN

I

THE BOY OF CADORE

THE boy's eyes were dark as the hearts of the daisies he carried, and they gazed wistfully after the horseman who was dashing along the white highway.

"Think of it, Catarina!" he exclaimed. "He rides to the wonderful city."

Catarina looked at her brother as if she did not understand. There were many towns along the road that ribboned away to the south, each of which seemed large indeed to the mountain girl, yet she had never thought of them as wonderful.

"The wonderful city?" she repeated. "Where is that, Tiziano?"

"Why, don't you know?" he asked in surprise. "As if it could be other than Venice, the great city of St. Mark!"

But the name did not thrill black-eyed Catarina. Older than her brother, and far less of a dreamer, she had heard that dreadful things happened in the city, and that sometimes people went hungry there. In the mountains there was food enough and to spare, and though no one was rich and lived in palaces with tapestried walls and gorgeous furnishings, neither were there any very poor. So she shrugged her shoulders and replied: "Oh, Venice! I don't know why you call that wonderful. Graziano, the weaver, has been there many times, and he thinks it not half as nice as our own Cadore. There are no mountains there, nor meadows where wild flowers grow. Are you tired of the Dolomites, Tiziano?"

"Ah, no!" came the earnest reply. "But the artists live in the city, and if I could go there, I might study with Bellini, and paint some of the things that are in my heart."

Catarina was just a practical village girl, who thought that if one had enough to eat and wear, he ought to be satisfied. So her

voice was chiding and a bit impatient as she answered.

"You talk so much about painting, and seeing things no one else sees, that the villagers say unless you get over your dreaming ways, you will grow up to be of no account. That is why Father thinks of apprenticing you to Luigi, the cobbler. For he can teach you his trade, which would be far better than always thinking about Venice. For, Tiziano, there are other things in the world beside painting."

Tiziano shook his head, but did not reply. Nothing else mattered half so much to him, and many a night, when the rest of the family were sleeping, he lay in his bed wondering how he could persuade his father to let him go away to study. It was well known that he spent many hours drawing on boards, stones, and anything he could find, and that the village priest, the good padrone, had praised his work. But little was thought of that. Other youths of Cadore had sketched as well and amounted to nothing. So why should he be sent to the city just because he could copy a mountain or a bit of woodland?

8   BOYHOOD STORIES

For he could not make them understand that color was what seemed to burn in his soul, because that he could not express with charcoal.

A whistle came from down the road, and Catarina saw her brother Francesco beckoning them to hurry.

"They must be ready to begin weaving the garlands!" she exclaimed.

So they broke into a run toward the village inn.

It was the glowing, fragrant June time of the Italian highlands, when the hillsides and meadows of the fertile Dolomite valleys were masses of many colored bloom, and next day the Festival of Flowers was to take place. They had spent the afternoon blossom hunting, and now, when sunset was crimsoning the peaks, were homeward bound with their spoils, to aid in preparing for the revelry.

In a few minutes, they joined the other young people at the inn, and began making garlands, and planning games and frolics as they worked. Pieve di Cadore was very far from the world in those days of little travel, and when the time of a festival was at hand,

THE BOY OF CADORE 9

the villagers were as light-hearted as the gay Venetians at carnival time. Songs and merry jests went round, and bits of gossip were told to eager listeners.

"Have you heard that Salvator, the miller's son, is going to Venice to study the art of carving?" asked a girl whose tongue kept pace with her hands. "Since his father has become rich, he has given up the idea of having him follow his own trade, and thinks it more elegant to become a sculptor. At first, Salvator did n't fancy it, but when told that an artist may get to be the favorite of a great lord or even of the doge himself, he was much pleased. Won't it be splendid if he becomes a noted man and lives in a fine house? Then we can say, 'Why, he is one of our Cadorini!'"

Sebastiano, whose uncle was a lawyer's clerk in Bergamo, and who knew more of city ways than the other village youths, remarked: "I did n't know he had the love of carving. It takes something beside a rich father to make an artist."

The talkative girl tossed her head.

"That may be!" she retorted. "But no

money, no masters; and without them, pray, how can one do anything?"

"So I tell Tiziano when he talks about going to the city to study painting," Catarina broke in. "Father is not rich, and it would be better for him to think about learning cobbling with Luigi."

Peals of laughter followed the announcement, and some one called out, "Tiziano! Why, he has n't had even a drawing-master. He builds the tower of his castle before he makes the foundation."

Tiziano's face turned very red. He had no teacher, it was true. But he believed he could prove he was worth one if given a chance.

"Oh, if I only had some paints!" he thought. "Maybe they would stop calling me a dreamer, for I am sure I could make a picture, and then perhaps I could go."

But pigments were rare and costly, and though his father was a well-to-do mountaineer, he had no gold to waste in buying colors for a lad who had never been taught to use them, and of course would spoil them.

The next morning, the boy noticed stains

on the stone walk made by flowers crushed there the day before. They were bright and fresh as if painted, and it put an idea into his head. He did not speak of it, however, although it was on his mind so much that, when the gaily decked villagers danced on the green, he did not see them, but, as soon as a chance came, he crept from the revelers and went out into the meadows.

Catarina saw him go, and wondered what took him from the merriment. Her curiosity was greater than her desire for fun, so she followed, and overtook him just as he reached a hillside aglow with blossoms.

"What are you doing, Tiziano?" she called.

The boy looked up as if doubtful whether to tell or not. But he knew his sister loved him even though she did criticize his dreaming, and that she would keep his secret.

"I am going to paint a picture," he answered.

For a minute she stood and stared. Then, thinking he was teasing, she retorted: "Of course you are, without any paints!"

But his earnest face told he was not joking.

"I shall use blossoms," he continued, with a wonderful light in his eyes. "See, all the colors are here, and I have found that they will stain. I saw where they did it on the stone walk."

Catarina was not a dreamer like her brother, and never saw pictures where others found only a bit of color, but she believed that what he proposed to do was not impossible, for she too had noticed the stains on the stone. And she began to think that he must be a very bright lad, for no ordinary one would have thought of it, and that perhaps his wanting to go to Venice was not a wild idea after all. If it was a splendid thing for Salvator, the miller's son, to become a sculptor, would it not be more splendid for Tiziano to paint pictures, and might not Cadore be proud of him too? She had heard the padrone say that no undertaking that fills the heart is impossible to one who has patience and courage and persistence, and that help always comes to those who try to help themselves. So she decided to help Tiziano, even though it was only in the keep-

THE BOY OF CADORE 13

ing of his secret and the gathering of materials for the work.

So into the fragrant patches they went and began collecting blossoms of every hue —reds, pinks, blues, and purples such as sunset painted on the mountains, and warm yellows and lavenders that the boy saw in the pictures of his fancy. Then they hurried to an old stone house that stood on land owned by their father. It was a vacant house, seldom visited by the family, and never by the villagers, and there, where he would be safe from molestation, he was to paint the picture that they hoped would be the means of taking him to Venice.

Catarina wanted to stay and watch the work, but Tiziano objected.

"I don't want even you to see it until it is finished, because at first it will not seem like a picture."

So she went away and left him outlining with a bit of charcoal on the wall.

For many days afterward, whenever he could steal away without being noticed, he worked with his flower paints. Catarina went over the meadows on feet that seemed to be winged, always watching that none of the villagers saw her put the blossoms in at the window near which her brother worked. So, while each petal made only a tiny stain, and the boy painted with the rapidity of one inspired, he not once needed to stop for materials.

Little by little the picture grew beneath the magic of his touch, and he and Catarina kept the secret well. Only the flocks pasturing on the fragrant uplands went near the deserted house, so no one knew that a boy was at work there who was destined to win glory for Italy. Little did the villagers dream, as Catarina skipped over the meadows, that the blossoms she gathered were being put to an immortal use.

One evening, when the sun was dipping behind the peaks and the merry voices of shepherds homeward bound with their flocks sounded down from the heights, Tiziano stepped to the door of the house and called to his sister outside.

"It is finished, Catarina, and is the very best that I can do!"

She went dancing in, filled with joy that

THE BOY OF CADORE 17

the task was done; but when she stood in front of the picture, the merriment went out of her face, and she spoke in tones of reverence:

"Oh, Tiziano, a madonna!"

"Yes," he agreed. "A madonna and child, with a boy like me offering a gift. It is what was in my heart, Catarina."

For some minutes she stood there forgetting everything else in the beauty of the fresco. Then, thinking of what it would mean to her brother when the villagers knew he had done such a wonderful thing, she started out to spread the news.

"Come and see!" she called to Luigi, the cobbler, as she hurried past the door where he was sorting his leather. "Tiziano has painted a madonna on the walls of the old stone house."

Word travels fast when it goes by the tongues of villagers, and soon a group of folk moved toward the building where the lad waited. His father, coming down from a day's hunting in the mountains, saw them go, and followed, wondering what was the matter. But by the time he reached the place, such a crowd had gathered that he could not see the fresco.

Murmurs of "How did he do it!" "Where did he get his paints?" rose on all sides, and every one was so excited that the father could not find out why they were there. Then he heard Tiziano's voice: "I did it with flowers from the hillsides. Catarina gathered them while I worked."

Exclamations of amazement followed, and the village priest, the good padrone, spoke reverently: "With the juices of flowers! Il Divino Tiziano!"

Antonio Vecelli looked about him as if dazed, for he could not believe what he heard.

"Am I mad," he asked a villager who was standing close by, "or did the padrone call my Tiziano 'the divine'?"

"No," came the answer. "You are not mad."

And when they told him the story, and the crowd stepped back that he might see, he, too, thought it a wonderful thing.

Whether or not Salvator, the miller's son, went to the city to study sculpture, no one

THE BOY OF CADORE 19

knows. But Tiziano did go, and the boy of Cadore became the marvel of Venice. There, guided by the master hand of Bellini, he began plying the brushes that were busy for almost eighty years, painting pictures whose glorious coloring has never been equaled, and proving to the mountain folk that it is n't bad, after all, to be a dreamer, for dreams combined with works do marvelous things.

That was back in the olden days, before Columbus sailed westward. But if the father, who thought he had gone mad when the village priest spoke his boy's name as reverently as he would a saint's, could come again to the valley of flowers in the Italian highlands, he would hear the selfsame words that were used that twilight time in speaking of his lad.

"Ecco!" the villagers say, as they point to a noble statue that looks out toward the meadows in which Catarina gathered blossoms for her brother, "Il Divino Tiziano.— See, the divine Titian!"

And by that name the world knows him to this very day.

WHEN MOZART RACED WITH
MARIE ANTOINETTE

II

WHEN MOZART RACED WITH MARIE ANTOINETTE

HE was the child of a poor musician, and she was an Austrian archduchess, yet they played as happily in the stately old garden as if there were no such thing in the world as high or low degree. The fountains around the grotto plashed and murmured, their falling waters meeting below the terraces in a stream that went singing away into the pines beyond; while from a pond half hidden in a riot of reeds and rushes, a speckled trout or silver-striped bass leaped up into the sunlight.

Wolfgang felt as if he had come to paradise, and it was not strange. The only garden in which he had ever played was the one at his home in Salzburg, where there was just a plot of grass and gnarled oak-tree, with a clump of yellow jasmine dipping over the old stone wall. A poor little garden, and suffering sometimes for the care his father and mother were both too busy to give it, while the great park at Schönbrunn, with its myriad singing-birds and acres and acres of grove and lawn, was the loveliest spot in all of lovely Austria.

"See!" he exclaimed, pointing to where a fountain threw out a veil of iridescent spray. "There is a rainbow there, just like the one we see in the sky after a shower."

Marie Antoinette nodded. To her the gleaming colors in the spray were an everyday sight.

"Of course," she replied; "there is always a rainbow where a fountain plays. It is great fun to run through the spray. Come, I'll beat you to the aspen-tree yonder."

And away they went, Marie's yellow curls flying, and merriment dancing in her wide, blue eyes. For a minute, Wolfgang kept even with her. But he was younger and less accustomed to exercise, for while the royal child spent the entire summer romping in the open, he sat at piano or harp practising for concerts that were a large source of the fam-

Away they went, Marie's yellow curls flying

WHEN MOZART RACED 27

ily income. His father was conductor of the court orchestra at Salzburg, and orchestra directors were paid little in those days, so Wolfgang and his sister Marianne, both of whom played wonderfully well, gave exhibitions of their skill, sometimes making as much on one of these occasions as did the elder Mozart in a month. But it meant many hours of practising, and bodies weaker than those of children who were free to romp and run. So Wolfgang began to fall behind, and Marie reached the goal several yards ahead of him.

"Oh!" she cried merrily. "I beat you, Wolfgang Mozart! I beat you, and I am a girl!"

Wolfgang bit his lip. It was bad enough to be vanquished by a girl without being taunted about it, and he felt like running away and hiding. But it was only for a minute. Then he realized that Marie had not meant to hurt him, for he knew her kind heart, and had not forgotten that, a few nights before, when he slipped and fell on the polished floor of the palace, instead of laughing with the others, she ran to help him up.

So what did it matter if she did boast about winning? She was big-hearted, and the pleasantest playmate he had ever had.

"Yes, Your Highness, you beat me at running," he answered, "but there is one kind of race in which you cannot."

Marie was alert with interest.

"What is it?" she asked.

"On the harp. You may play and I will play, and we will ask the Countess of Brandweiss who does best."

The little duchess clapped her hands. She was a fun-loving child, and always ready for a new form of sport.

"It will be splendid!" she cried. "And if you win, you may have my silver cross. But we must wait until to-morrow, for Mother will be out from Vienna then, and she will be a better judge than the Brandweiss. Let us go and practise now, so each one can do his best."

"But, Your Highness," came a voice from among the trees, "do not forget that you are the daughter of an empress."

It was the Countess of Brandweiss who spoke, and Marie Antoinette shrugged her

WHEN MOZART RACED 29

shoulders, for she knew very well what her governess meant.

Wolfgang was a boy of no rank, and but for the fact that Maria Theresa was a tender mother as well as a great empress, would not have been at Schönbrunn. But mothers think of the happiness of their children, and sometimes royal ones allow what queens alone would not.

So it happened that, when the Mozart children, who were on a concert tour with their father, played before the court at Vienna, and Marie Antoinette took a great fancy to the delicate-faced boy, the empress asked the musician to let his son spend a few days at Schönbrunn as the playmate of her daughter. It was an unusual honor for a lad of the people, and the Countess of Brandweiss was not at all sure that it was wise. That is why she objected to the contest. It seemed like putting them on an equality. But Marie Antoinette was too impulsive and kind to think much about such things, and reasoned that her mother intended them to play as they wished, or she would not have invited Wolfgang to Schönbrunn.

So they went toward the palace in high glee, the lad very sure of winning, and Marie almost as sure, for she had had music lessons ever since her fingers were strong enough to strum the strings, and one of the things she could do exceedingly well was to play on the harp. So both went to their practising, and by the time that was done, Marie had a French lesson with her governess, and Wolfgang spent the remainder of the afternoon in the park alone.

The next morning, every one about the palace was excited. The empress was coming early from Vienna, and her apartments always had to be decorated with flowers before her arrival. Marie and Wolfgang flew in and out among the workers, being really very much in the way, yet imagining they were helping. The young duchess was radiantly happy, and danced and sang. Maria Theresa was one of the world's greatest rulers, and affairs of state kept her so busy that she saw very little of her children, especially during the summer, when they were at Schönbrunn, away from the heat and dust of the city. Throughout that time, she visited them only once a week, and by Marie Antoinette, who thought her mother the loveliest woman in the world, the rare but joyous occasions upon which they were together were delightfully anticipated and joyously remembered. So it was not strange that she wanted a hand in beautifying the palace for the reception of its loved mistress.

A trumpet call from the warder at the outer gate announced the arrival of the empress, and the Countess of Brandweiss led Marie and her sister, the Archduchess Caroline, into the great hall to pay tribute to the royal mother. Wolfgang stayed behind with the attendants, for the strict etiquette of the Austrian court did not permit him to be present on such an occasion. He watched Maria Theresa embrace her daughters as lovingly as any mother who had never worn a crown, and thought, with Marie Antoinette, that she was the most beautiful woman in the world. She was so big, and fair, and splendidly handsome, and the mother-love gleamed tenderly in her clear, blue eyes.

After the greetings were over, she moved toward her apartments, and, seeing Wolfgang by the way, stopped and kissed him. Then all followed her to her reception-room, and Marie told of the race.

"But Wolfgang Mozart says he can beat me on the harp," she continued, "so we are going to find out. Your Majesty and Caroline and the Brandweiss shall be judges."

Maria Theresa smiled.

"It must be soon, then," she said, "for at eleven Baron Kaunitz comes to talk over some important matters."

"Oh!" exclaimed Marie, petulantly; "it is always Kaunitz who breaks in on our good times! I wish he would go so far away that it would take him a year to get back."

For a minute, Maria Theresa looked in amazement at her daughter. Then she spoke reprovingly, but gently:

"My child, Baron Kaunitz is Austria's great prime minister, and must be spoken of with respect by the daughter of Austria's empress."

The little duchess hung her head. She was not rude at heart, but just self-willed, and fond of having things go to suit her.

"I am sorry, Mother!" she cried, as she

WHEN MOZART RACED 33

flung her arms around the empress's neck. "I know he is good and great, but why does he take you from me so often?"

"Because public affairs demand it," the mother said, as she stroked the sunny curls, "and not because he is unkind. You must not fret about it, for princesses must consider many things besides their own desires. Let us be happy now, and not waste time with regrets. We will go to the hill above here—my favorite spot of all Schönbrunn. Then we shall see who plays best. Brandweiss, order the harp to be taken out, please."

The governess left the room to carry out her instructions, and Maria Theresa and the children went into the park. The wealth of flowers threw out mingled perfumes, and as they strolled along the shaded walks, among rare trees and by plashing fountains and statues, every one of which was the triumph of some great artist, Maria Theresa laughed and jested, stopping now to pick a flower or to glance over the housetops of Vienna to the Danube and the hills of the Wienerwald.

It was good to be free from public affairs for an hour—free, just like any ordinary mother, to stroll with her children and talk about books, and games, and pets, instead of puzzling over treaties with Frederick the Great, and questions of international friendship. And, as Wolfgang watched her stoop to look at a beetle or to crown Marie Antoinette with a daisy chain or laurel garland, he could hardly believe that this laughing woman was the stately ruler who presided over the destinies of the great Austrian land.

They lingered awhile at the zoölogical garden, and then went on past the labyrinth and the Neptune fountain to the eminence where now stands the Gloriette. A pretty rustic lodge crowned it in those days, and Maria Theresa loved the spot and spent many hours there.

Johann Michael, one of the house servants, arrived just as they did, and set the harp in its place. Then the Brandweiss came, and the empress gave the word for the contest to begin.

"You play, Maria Antoinetta," she said using the affectionate German name by which the little archduchess was called until negotiations were under way for her French

WHEN MOZART RACED 37

marriage. For no matter how gracious the mother might be to the musician's child, the Empress of Austria must observe the rules of court etiquette, one of which was that princesses must always take precedence over those of lower rank.

The girl began, and wonderfully well she played. No one knew it better than Wolfgang, and as her white fingers danced along the strings, he listened in real admiration, while Maria Theresa thought with pride that few of her age could do as well. When she finished, the judges and the boy who was her competitor broke into genuine applause, and the Brandweiss smiled with gratification at her charge, very sure that, although Wolfgang had often played in public, he could not do as well. The countess had very decided opinions about things, and was particularly strong in her belief that low-born children ought not to be allowed to vie with princesses of the blood royal.

"Now, Master Mozart," the Archduchess Caroline said, "you take the harp, and see if you can do better."

Wolfgang moved to the instrument and

38 BOYHOOD STORIES

swept his fingers across the strings. First came a few broken chords, and then an exquisite strain of melody, a folk-song of old Austria still to be heard at eventide in the fields around Salzburg, as the peasants come in from their toiling. Caroline sat with clasped hands and gleaming eyes. She had listened to that ballad many times, but never had it seemed so beautiful. The empress, very still, looked far out across the sweep of hill and plain that skirted the river, her face wonderfully tender as she listened to the gifted child. Even the punctilious countess forgot her prejudices, and looked at the boy with misty eyes, for the melody took her back to the far-off time when as a child on an old estate at Salzburg she had often sat with her mother and listened to peasant songs sweetening the twilight. Again she saw the flowers and trees of the well-remembered park, the hunting lodge and the copsewood just beyond, and heard the voice of her father, who had slept for years among Austria's honored dead.

But Wolfgang thought only of the music, and played as seldom a child has played,

WHEN MOZART RACED

something stronger and finer than his will guiding his sensitive fingers along the strings.

The melody died away, and he turned to his listeners with a question in his eyes. He was so eager to win, yet he knew the young archduchess had done remarkably well.

But Marie Antoinette did not wait for the word of the judges. She ran to him in her big-hearted, impulsive way, and pinned the cross on his coat.

"You have beaten me," she said, "and the cross is yours! You have won it, Wolfgang, for I cannot play *half* as well as that!"

An attendant appeared just then and saluted the empress.

"Your Majesty," he announced, "his excellency, the Baron Kaunitz awaits your commands at the palace."

But Maria Theresa, mighty ruler of the Austrian land, seemed not to hear. She had forgotten all about affairs of state, and sat as one in a dream, charmed by the magical music of Mozart, as men and women are still charmed by it to-day.

THE TOMBOY FROM BORDEAUX

III

THE TOMBOY FROM BORDEAUX

"YOU think you have a daughter, mv Sophia, but you are mistaken, for Rosalie is not a girl. She is just a boy in petticoats!"

Madame Bonheur looked up from her spinning with a smile that was tinged with sadness, for she knew her father spoke the truth, and it grieved her. But a musical laugh floated into the room just then, and her eyes turned lovingly toward the girl who was romping under the chestnut-trees.

"It seems that way," she replied, "and I often wish she were different. But she has a clear mind and a good heart, and I think will come out all right."

"Aye, aye, I hope so," the old man said, as he walked to the door and looked out at the sky against whose midsummer blue were painted the masts of a hundred ships. The

Bonheurs lived not far from the Bordeaux docks, and between the trees might always be had a glimpse of the vessels anchored there; so he stood with a pleasant expression on his wrinkled face, listening to the calls of the men who were working among the boats.

Madame Bonheur went on with her household tasks, now turning from the spinning to tend the stew that simmered over the charcoal fire, or to turn the square of linen bleaching just outside the window, and wondering much, as she threw the creamy tow over the spindle, what made her Rosalie so different from other girls, always wanting to romp with boys instead of doing a stint of embroidery as a French maiden should.

But out in the pleasant garden Rosalie was having a beautiful time. No thought of anything but the game of soldier they were playing was in her mind, for she was captain, and the fighters who followed her were her brother Auguste and a group of neighborhood children, charging and retreating against a fort—which was n't a fort at all, but just a stone wall over which pale pink roses tumbled in a mass of bloom. They sal-

The grandfather stood by the stone gate calling good-by as they drove away

TOMBOY FROM BORDEAUX 47

lied and skirmished as if each one were a chevalier of France, and of course there was victory for the assaulting army. For no death-dealing guns thundered from that rampart, and it was easy to become a general or even a field-marshal through victories gained so quickly and easily. Perhaps many a battle might have been waged in that one short afternoon, but a call from the door sent military tactics out of the young commander's head. The neighborhood children scurried homeward, and with Auguste at her heels she scampered toward the house, leaving the wall and its roses to sleep in the sunshine as before.

"Your father is there, and he has something to tell you," the mother announced as they ran into the low-ceiled room. "See if you can guess what it is."

And the two climbed up on his chair, begging to be told all about it.

"I know!" Auguste exclaimed, as he clapped his small brown hands. "You 're going to take us to the docks to see the boats."

He was always thinking of the harbor and of the sturdy seamen who sang as they toiled there, and could imagine nothing more delightful than an hour along the quays.

But Rosalie shook her head.

She loved animals as few children loved them, and was not, like Auguste, wild about the boats and the sailors.

"Of course not!" she said merrily. "I think he means to get us another dog, or maybe a goat."

At which the father and mother both laughed.

"Neither of you has guessed rightly," the man spoke pleasantly. "I am going to Paris, and after a while will send for you, and we shall all be Parisians."

Auguste gave a scream of delight.

"Oh, I am so glad!" he cried. "There are hundreds of soldiers in Paris, and Emile, the tailor's son, told me that sometimes the river there is white with boats. I wish we might go to-day."

Rosalie did not seem so eager about it. Paris was very large, and many people there had no yards at all. There might not be room for the dogs and cats and pets she liked so much, and it seemed better to stay in Bor-

TOMBOY FROM BORDEAUX 49

deaux. But if the city was to be their home, it would be well to learn something more about it. So she questioned in an earnest voice, "May I take my rabbits and Smoke and the five little cats?"

The mother smiled and shook her head.

"No, dear. But so many wonderful things are in the city that it will seem very fine to be there even without your pets."

Rosalie thought her mother very wise, and if she said a thing it must be so. Perhaps it would not be bad in Paris, after all. So she began to be quite excited about it, and watched eagerly while the small green trunk was packed. It seemed almost like a picnic, for she was too young to understand how hard it was for her father to leave Bordeaux, and that he was going away only because his income as a teacher in the southern town would not reach to cover all their needs, while in the city there was a chance of making more money.

Next day, they stood under the chestnut-trees and watched him go down the road and out of sight, the mother and Pépé, the grandfather, with tearful eyes, for they realized what struggle the coming days might hold for him. But Rosalie and Auguste were smiling. Their thoughts were that, some day, they, too, would drive away in the post-chaise to see the wonders of Paris, and perhaps, if the mother had not put them to other things, would have talked about it the rest of the day. But there were lessons to be prepared. So they sat down under the trees with their reading-books. But Rosalie did n't study long. Almost before she realized what she was doing, she took out her slate and began to draw.

Grandfather Bonheur walked through the garden a little later, and by that time old Smoke, the gray house-cat, was copied on the red-framed slate.

"Ah, lass!" he exclaimed, as he looked at it. "If you put in the time drawing when you should be at your lessons, you will grow up an ignoramus."

Rosalie caught his hand with an impulsive caress.

"I forgot, Pépé!" she said. "I'll study."

And she turned again to her book while the old man walked on.

TOMBOY FROM BORDEAUX 51

"The maid surely has a gift when it comes to using her pencil," he murmured as he went; "and if she'd get her lessons as well as she draws, she'd amount to something some day."

For little did he dream that her drawing was destined to cast undying honor on the Bonheur name.

A year passed, and the father sent for them to come to Paris. Then what excitement there was in the old house! Pépé, the grandfather, felt that he was too old to make new friends and learn city ways, so he decided to stay behind with some relatives. But he helped with the preparations, and stood by the stone gate calling good-by as they drove away. Madame Bonheur could not keep back the tears at the thought of leaving him, and the chestnut-trees, and the harbor, with its gray-masted boats, and Rosalie's lip quivered as she gave old Smoke a farewell hug. But Auguste was excited over the thought of the new life that was to begin for them in the city, and called back gaily in answer to the good-bys.

"It is a shabby house," Raymond Bonheur

said when he took them to their new home; "very dingy and dull-looking, and not pretty like the one in Bordeaux. But we must stay here until I get to earning more. Then we can move to better quarters."

Rosalie agreed with him. It seemed very cold and dreary after the sunshine and clear skies of the southland, and she wanted to be back in the old harbor town, where finches held revel in the chestnut-trees, and roses ran riot over the brown wall. But after a while the strangeness of things interested her, and she forgot her homesickness.

A few days later, the father announced that he had a chance to send her to a schoolmaster.

"His name is Monsieur Antin," he explained, "and he has only boys. But Rosalie gets along so well with them, that he says he will take her, and it will be good for her to be with Auguste."

Rosalie was delighted.

"I like that!" she said. "Boys' games just suit me, for I love to play soldier and fight sham battles."

So to Monsieur Antin's school she went,

TOMBOY FROM BORDEAUX 53

and joined in the games with such a zest that she came to be known all along the street as "The Tomboy from Bordeaux." If there was a sham battle, she was in the lead, and, as it seemed quite silly for a soldier to be called Rosalie, her name was shortened to Rosa, by which she was known from that time forth.

Then came the revolution of 1830, with guns thundering almost at the Bonheur door. The Place de la Bastille was not far away, and while it was being stormed, Rosa narrowly escaped being the victim of a cannon discharge. Troubled days followed, and the family moved to a smaller and cheaper house, far from the home that had now grown very dear to them. Attendance at Monsieur Antin's school ended, and Rosa's only playmates were her brothers, Auguste and Isidore, and a little girl named Natalie. But her nickname followed to the new home, and she was still known as "The Tomboy from Bordeaux."

Several years passed, and she was now a big girl. She did very little studying, but a great deal of drawing and painting, sometimes earning a few sous coloring prints for a man who lived near by. The mother had died, and ' Monsieur Bonheur, himself a scholar, could not bear to think of his daughter growing up in ignorance. So once more she was sent to school, this time with about a hundred girls, to Madame Gilbert's Institute, where they were expected to become dignified and proper young ladies. But Rosa could n't be dignified, no matter how hard she tried. Always she had been a tomboy, and if the old grandfather in Bordeaux could have seen her now, he would still have said that she was just a boy in petticoats.

Madame Gilbert was very dignified and very proper. When she stood up, she did it in just the right manner, and when she sat down, it was so correctly that the most careful person could not criticize. Her heart was n't quite as big as Rosa's, and every animal about the place would run from the mistress at the call of the dark-haired tomboy. But that did n't seem to matter. Her mission was to make polished and proper Parisians, and she had little patience with a girl who wanted to be anything else. Even

The room that was her workshop came to be a sort of Noah's Ark

TOMBOY FROM BORDEAUX 57

Rosa's love of animals and her delight in drawing them displeased the mistress, who scolded her for not making pictures of flowers, which was far more ladylike. But Rosa drew the things that were in her heart, and it was good for the world she did. Madame Gilbert, however, couldn't understand that, and kept wishing for a chance to send the tomboy home.

At last it came.

The girls were all out in the garden, and, as usual, Rosa was brimming over with good nature.

"Let's have a sham battle!" she called.

And immediately they were organized into a company.

Sticks of wood made splendid sabers, and as the young commander ordered a cavalry charge, they rushed with vim toward the rose garden.

But the battle was never finished. Madame Gilbert's shrill voice rang out just then, and Captain Rosa was ignominiously locked in a closet. Such an indignity was unheard of in a well-regulated school, and the next day her father came and took her home, having given up all hope of polishing her into a proper young lady.

But he remembered her mother's words, "She has a clear mind and a good heart, and must come out all right;" and, because he knew she loved drawing, was wise enough to let her work at it all she pleased, and fitted up a room for her studio. Sometimes she went to the Louvre to study the masterpieces there, for every gem in that great treasure-house was a delight to her. But the animal pictures appealed to her most strongly, and these she copied with wonderful skill. Sometimes on Sunday, with her father and his good friend, Justin Mathieu, the famous sculptor, she went far into the country, wandering off wherever she saw cattle or horses or sheep. They seemed to sense her love of them and came near, always receiving a warm caress. The sculptor recognized her marvelous skill in portraying them, and urged her father to let her have as many pets as she could keep. So the room that was her workshop came to be a sort of Noah's ark, where rabbits, tame squirrels, ducks, and quail held revel, and canaries and finches flew

TOMBOY FROM BORDEAUX

in and out. Then some one gave her a goat, and, with her dogs and cats, she had a real menagerie.

But still she was the tomboy. She loved games as well as she loved painting, and perhaps because she played so hard is one reason why she painted so well.

"I want to study other animals," she said one day to her father; "cattle, instead of just the horses I see in the street and the little creatures I have here at home."

And Raymond Bonheur was perplexed. One does not see cattle in city streets, and they had no pennies to spare to pay board in the country. But Rosa found a way. She went where the animals were taken that were brought to Paris for the markets, and here she made dozens of sketches which were afterwards transferred to canvas. Once a circus came to Paris, and when the owner heard of the girl who painted animals so wonderfully, he gave her permission to work in his menagerie as long as it stayed in the city, and there, day after day, she sketched the lions, tigers, and other creatures of foreign lands.

When one is busy, the time seems to go on wings, and, before she realized it, years had passed, and her work was known far and wide, and recognized as something very remarkable. Even Landseer, then the world's master-painter of animals, could not portray them in a more lifelike manner than the young Frenchwoman. They seemed ready to step from her canvases and move about the fields and roadsides, for she put love into her work, and infinite patience too. Years were spent over her marvelous "Horse Fair"; years, too, on its great companion piece, "Coming from the Fair," and every hour of the time was richly worth while, for they will gladden the hearts of beauty lovers for hundreds of years to come.

The old studio with its rabbits and birds and goat had been abandoned, for by this time Rosa's work was earning so much money that she could afford a great estate in the fresh, green country, and all the animals she wanted. So in the forest of Fontainebleau she made a home spot, where she lived and worked. Her fame spread to every

TOMBOY FROM BORDEAUX 61

land, and there was none too great to honor the tomboy from Bordeaux.

For tomboy she was still. She never grew too old to join in a game with children, or too far away from the sham battles and cavalry charges of her youth to refuse to organize a company. The girls from Madame Gilbert's school had become dignified and proper Parisian dames, who dressed beautifully and drove in the boulevards as dignified ladies do. But nobody ever heard of them. While, wherever beauty was loved, Rosa, who most of the time wore a denim jumper and short skirt, was known as a wonder-worker.

One day she was busy over a sketch, when her companion rushed into the studio in great excitement, exclaiming: "Madame, the Empress is here!"

Rosa Bonheur had on her usual working attire, rather a queer costume in which to receive the Empress of France. But that mattered little to beautiful Eugénie. She knew of the glory the artist was winning for her land, and had come to give her homage.

"It is the Cross of the Legion of Honor,"

she said as she held up a glittering emblem. "You have won it, and deserve to wear it."

Tears came into Rosa's dark eyes. She knew that was the highest honor that could come to a child of France, and that the greatest ambition of the most illustrious men of many generations had been to win that guerdon.

So she went on, trying to be worthy of it, working hard and being happy because she was leading a good and useful life.

And, besides putting beauty into the world, her work accomplished other big things. Men grew kinder to animals because of her paintings, and in several cities they led to laws being passed to make easier the lives of dumb creatures.

So, although it does seem strange for a girl to fight sham battles and lead cavalry charges, there are worse things in the world than being a tomboy, if she has a clear mind and a good heart, like Rosa Bonheur.

JACOPO, THE LITTLE DYER

IV

JACOPO, THE LITTLE DYER

HE was a handsome lad, strong-limbed and sturdy, and although dressed in the dun-colored smock worn only by Venetian youths of low degree, was as happy as if his father had been one of the Council of Ten. For it was sunset time; and from the balcony of the dim apartment that served as the family living-room, he could look out on the canal, flushed then with glorified light.

A girl with laughing eyes, and hands purple-stained from the dye-pots, came running into the room and called his name. But he did not turn, because he did not hear. He was too busy with his thoughts for familiar sounds to disturb him, for just then everything except the beauty of the shimmering lagoon was crowded out of his mind, and he saw only the amethysts and opals that flashed at every ripple.

The girl was not held spellbound by the wizardry of the sunset. She was just a child of the tintori (the dyers), and she never had fancies beyond those of the money the dyeing would bring, and the trinkets she might buy, and thought it far better to talk of the good fortune come to them that day, than to stand gazing out on the canal. So she went up and shook him violently.

"Jacopo!" she exclaimed. "Jacopo Robusti! Wake up, boy! Don't you know that this is a great day for us? Now that the Dogaressa has sent her goods to be colored, other great folk are sure to patronize this shop, and before long your father will be the most prosperous dyer in Venice. Surely you know that, Jacopo!"

The boy turned slowly, as if reluctant to take his eyes from the glowing canal. For now that the heat was over, gondolas were beginning to glide by, and snatches of song came from the lips of the light-hearted rowers. The music, the color, and the swan-like motion of the boats belonged together, and Jacopo loved it all. But no matter how strong its allurement, it could not hold him

JACOPO, THE LITTLE DYER

after his cousin came into the room. For she was a persistent maid, and always kept nagging until she had her way.

"I know," he replied, "and also that the work must be ready to-morrow night, which means that I'll have to stay at home and help, instead of going out on the Canalezzo to see the sunset."

Floria frowned at him.

"The idea of thinking of anything but your father's good fortune!" she rebuked. "The sun goes down every night, and the canal will always be there. But we've never had work from the Dogaressa before, and you ought to be glad to stay at home and lend a hand. Come and look at the stuff. It is silk from the Indies, and will be colored crimson."

The odor of boiling dye came in through the open door, and his father's voice called just then. Jacopo knew there was no more standing on the balcony for him, so he followed Floria into the shop that, its walls gay with pictures in fresco fashion, adjoined the living-room; and soon they were at work grinding the colors that were to transform the creamy silk of the Indies into a gorgeous crimson fit for the court robe of a Venetian lady. Robusti the elder was rolling up some material colored that day, while the apprentice tintori, their arms mottled from the dipping, were finishing up the last bit of work. Dust from the grinding pigments and steam from the boiling vats filled the place; and as Jacopo worked, he thought how pleasant it must be on the canal, with odors from many a walled garden wafting across it, and the soft singing of lithe-limbed gondoliers. But he was a true Venetian lad, and, when the father spoke, had no thought save that of obedience. That is why the walls were so brightly tinted. For often when his heart was out on the lagoons and he had to stay at home and help, he filled the intervals between watching the pots and turning the coloring fabrics by making charcoal sketches and tinting them with dyes.

There were dozens of such pictures; here a bit of sea with a sunset sky like a painted canopy above the white-sailed galleys, and there a lord of Venice, gaily robed as Venetian nobles were in those golden days.

JACOPO, THE LITTLE DYER 69

Scattered among them were groups of tintori, like his father and his father's men, with dye-bespattered arms, and smocks as many colored as Joseph's coat, and sometimes there were snatches of fairy landscape across which fantastic figures flitted, just as in the pictures of his fancy. For when the soul is as full of beautiful things as an overflowing river, some of them are sure to get out where people will see.

The next morning every member of the Robusti household was up before the ringing of the matin-bells. The apprentice tintori came early too, and soon the pots were steaming and a hum of work was about the shop. For the silk had been promised for that evening, and to disappoint the Dogaressa would be ruinous indeed. It would mean that never again would great folk patronize the place, and that would be a calamity, for great folk paid well. So all hands worked with a vim, the men turning and stirring while the dyer directed, Jacopo and Floria both lending a hand. There was water to be brought, and refuse liquor to be carried away, which they could do as well as any one.

Evening came and all was finished, and although Jacopo had not had a chance to go out on the canal, he was so interested that he forgot to be disappointed. The costume-maker who was coming to pass upon the work might arrive any minute, and Jacopo wanted to hear what he had to say. Of course it was perfectly done, but so much depended upon the success of that dyeing that all looked forward eagerly to hearing the words of approval.

"How splendid it will be when he says it is all right!" Floria exclaimed, as she danced around the table where the sheeny stuff was piled in crimson billows. "Word will go out all over Venice, and nobles will give us their patronage."

And Robusti the elder smiled at her, for he knew that she spoke the truth. But Jacopo said nothing. He was busy drawing on the wall.

Sweetly across the lagoons the Angelus sounded, and for a minute all was quiet in the shop. Jacopo paused from his drawing, and laughing-eyed Floria did not finish her dance, for always those of the Robusti house-

JACOPO, THE LITTLE DYER 71

hold were faithful in their devotions, and because of gratitude over their good fortune they were more fervid than usual.

Then the inspector came, with pompous bearing and speech abounding in high-sounding words, pronouncing the work perfect, and the Robusti family knew it was the beginning of wonderful things for them. But one blessing it brought of which they had not dreamed, beside which the glory of dyeing the Dogaressa's robe was poor indeed. That faded and wore out, but the other glory, that had its beginning that day, has lasted through five hundred years. For as the inspector turned to go, he saw the figures on the wall.

"Oh, ho!" he exclaimed. "A gay shop you have here. And who is the merry painter, pray?"

Robusti the elder answered in words of apology.

"I do not wonder that you think such walls unfit for a dignified business, and assure you that it is none of my doing. My boy Jacopo defaced them when he had better have been thinking of his trade."

Jacopo turned his wide dark eyes on the man, wondering if he too would reprove him because of his picture-making. He had been scolded so often for wasting his time, and supposed of course the costume-maker would share the family opinion. But he met with a surprise.

"That sturdy chap yonder?" the man asked. "I've a knowledge of pictures, and this work seems from the hand of one well-nigh grown."

"I did it," Jacopo answered, "but not because I wanted to spoil the shop. I had no other place."

The inspector shook his head.

"I would not have believed it!" he said. "Surely he has the gift."

Then to the father:

"Mayhap your lad will become a good dyer, but he will make a far better artist; and if you are wise, you will set about apprenticing him to a painter. There is Titian of Cadore, the flower of Venetian colorists. Before another day passes, I would see him and beg that he try the boy."

Robusti the dyer was a sensible man. Al-

Jacopo began his work with the Master

JACOPO, THE LITTLE DYER 75

though there were no horses in Venice, he had lived in Ravenna once, and knew if a steed is built for speed and much travel, it is a mistake to set him to drawing loads. And he was wise enough to realize that, if one has a gift for painting, it is sad indeed to keep him in a dye-shop. The inspector's word meant much, and, as he thought the boy should become an artist, it must be true. So it was decided to place him with a master.

"He shall have a chance to do his best," the father said, as they talked it over that night, "for it shall not be charged to me that I spoiled a good painter to make a second-rate dyer."

The next morning Jacopo and his father set out for the workshop of Titian of Cadore. The pearl-gray of dawn was still over the city, but, through the open spaces between the buildings, reflected rays from the out-peeping sun reached arms of light along the canals. Across the Piazza of San Marco they went, under the clock-tower whose two bronze giants glowed and shimmered, and into the Merceria, where there was a Babel of sound as the merchant folk opened their shops. But they did not stop to look at the pretty things nor to gossip with the loiterers gathered there, although the boy would have liked to pause a bit before the pictures the men on the benches were painting. But there was no time to lose, as the dyer must soon return to his shop. So straight on they went, across the curving Rialto and down the narrow street beyond, where, taking a boat, they came to the studio of the master.

"Will you try the boy?" the dyer asked, as he explained that the worthy costume-maker himself had recommended a painter's career for him. And in answer the great man told him to come next day and begin work.

Jacopo's heart sang all the way home, and he worked in the shop that afternoon as he had never worked before. For even though he did not like the half-sickening odors and the perpetual steaming of the boiling liquid, he knew he would enter a wonder-world on the morrow, and until that time things disagreeable mattered little. Floria had never seen him so gay, and remarked to her uncle

JACOPO, THE LITTLE DYER

that he was surely the happiest boy in Venice.

"It shows he can be contented at dyeing," she said.

For still she believed that to be of the tintori was better than to be a painter.

But the man shook his head.

"No," he replied, "it is the thought of what is to come that makes him glad."

Jacopo began his work with the master, and Heaven seemed to have opened its gates to him. Titian then had many canvases in his workshop, and the beauty-loving lad drank in the magic of their coloring as thirsty travelers drink from cooling springs, his eyes reveling in the gold and purples and crimsons that surpassed everything he had ever seen except the sunset tints on the lagoons. The working days in the studio were long, yet he was never glad when they came to an end, and always looked eagerly to the beginning of another. It was an enchanted land in which he dwelt, and he was a fairy prince.

But his joy was to be short-lived, for very soon afterward the master sent him away. Why, no one knows, although many guesses have been made as to the reason, and some have gone so far as to say that Titian was jealous of the gifted youth and feared he might eclipse him. But it does not seem possible that the master-painter of Italy could have feared a mere boy, for he was great enough to know that there is room in the world for more than one genius. But at any rate he sent him away, and dark days began for Jacopo.

Many a lad would have given up and gone back to the dye-shop, but not Robusti's son. He was made of the stuff that wins, and every obstacle in his way goaded him on to greater effort. The greatest master of Venice had refused to teach him. But he determined to teach himself, and the struggle he had in doing it has never been equaled by an artist before or since.

Along the Merceria were elevated benches where the poorer painters sat and did their work before the eyes of the passing throng, selling it sometimes while the canvases were still wet. There Jacopo went day after day, to watch them mix and apply the colors. Once he worked with journeymen printers at

JACOPO, THE LITTLE DYER 79

San Marco, and once with stone-masons at Cittadella that he might learn the principles of joining. To know the laws of proportion, he watched the people in the streets and modeled them in wax, moving these figures back and forth between lamps to watch the effect of the shadows.

For ten years he struggled on, always studying, always watching and working. It would have been easier to have taken up his father's trade, for in the dye-shop, when the day's toil is over, there follows a night of rest. But Jacopo thought only of being a painter, and was bound to succeed. So he kept on. All the work that paid well was given to Titian, and that Jacopo might get his pictures where people could see them, he had to paint for nothing. But that did not matter. He was learning and growing, and at last he had his day.

Titian died, and all Venice wondered who would take his place.

"There is no one else," the critics said sadly. "His like will not come again."

But one of the nobles who was wise enough to know that when a work is to be done there is always a man to do it, thought of Jacopo Robusti.

"Why not Tintoretto?" asked this one, whose word was law. And by Tintoretto he meant Jacopo, who because of his father's trade was called "The Little Dyer."

"We will go and see," they said. "And it will be a glad day if he can take the master's place."

So the great of Venice gathered about the paintings of one who had given his work to every church and building that would receive it. In Santa Maria della Orto they found it, in shops along the Merceria, and out Treviso way in village churches where peasants met to worship.

"It is wonderful!" they exclaimed. "What magnificent coloring! What perfection of line! Surely this is the work of the master."

For they did not know that, during the years they had scorned him, his one thought and one aim had been to make his pictures as fine as Titian's, and he had succeeded so well that they mistook them for the master's.

Then it was agreed that he should paint in

JACOPO, THE LITTLE DYER 81

the Doge's Palace, the greatest honor that could come to a Venetian artist. And there he left much work that still draws to the city of St. Mark art lovers from every quarter of the globe. There is his exquisite "Adoration of the Savior," and there too is the wonderful "Paradise," the largest oil-painting in the world.

But Venice is not the only city that is rich in his handiwork. Many galleries in many lands have given princely sums to obtain it, and his canvases have been carried to France and Germany, and even to the banks of the Thames, where, in the stately halls they adorn, they give joy to thousands, although the hand that fashioned them has been still for five hundred years. Yet very few know the name of Jacopo Robusti, because to this day, as in the old Venetian time, he is still called in the musical tongue of the lagoons, "Tintoretto,—The Little Dyer."

BARTOLOME'S VELVET HAT

V

BARTOLOME'S VELVET HAT

BLACK-EYED Bartolome Murillo was the happiest child in Seville. No more insults and times of disgrace for him, he thought; no more taunts from his playmates about being a baby because he wore the cap that was the headgear of very small Spanish children. He had a hat now, with a peaked crown and rolling brim, and because it was made of the finest velvet and trimmed with a silver band to match his suit, old Carmalita, who lived next door, said he looked like a young cavalier. It is a dreadful thing to be called a baby when one feels quite a big boy, and as the cap was responsible for the title it was little wonder he was glad to put it aside.

"You are big enough to stop wearing the nino[1] cap," his mother said when she gave

[1] Nino—baby.

it to him as his birthday gift that morning. "You shall have a hat like a man."

And Bartolome was more glad than he had ever been, for as long as one wears *nino* clothes he is sure to be called a *nino,* and he was tired of it.

He went out into the street to look if any of his playmates were about, but not one was in sight, for it was August, when the sun shines with burning heat in southern Spain, and boys are fond of seeking the cool of the river. He wanted them to know that his cap belonged to the past, and that he could be called a baby no longer because of his clothes, so he started out to look for them.

The heat had driven most of the people into the houses, which made Bartolome sorry, for he was so proud of the new hat that he would have liked all the world to see. He was sure they would think it as lovely as he did, although that was a very great mistake, for at that time such headgear was quite in fashion in Spain, and created no more of a sensation than Panamas do to-day. But he was too young to realize it, and whenever he passed a lady in her carriage, or a

BARTOLOME'S VELVET HAT 89

gaudily skirted market-girl with a red rose glowing in her shining black hair, he saluted with the air of a grandee. He did not see his friends, although he went far down the street, past gardens sweet with the breath of oleanders, and beyond the cathedral and the Giralda that rises like a fairy tower beside it, to the bridge that spans the Guadalquiver; for while he was rejoicing over his present, they had scattered about the city. So he turned back, reaching home just as his mother was ready to start to church.

"You stay here until I get back," she said as she adjusted her lace mantilla on her head and fastened it at the shoulders with golden clasps. "Your Aunt Eulalia may come at any time, and she must not be greeted by closed doors."

Bartolome had meant to get something to eat and go out into the street again, yet he did not mind much when told to stay at home. To have a wish come true as he had had that morning is enough to make the day bright, even if everything else does not come one's way. So putting the beloved hat on the table where he could see it, he began wondering what to do until his mother returned.

Just above him on the wall was a picture of a child and a lamb, which, ever since he could remember, had been in that place. It was faded and stained by time, for it had hung in his mother's girlhood home before being brought into his own, and was one of the treasured possessions of the house of Murillo. As he looked at the bare-headed lad and then at his birthday present, he thought he would like it better if the boy had a hat like his own.

"And I'd rather play with a dog than a lamb," he thought. "I guess whoever painted that picture did n't know much about boys. I'm going to fix it."

So taking a piece of charcoal, he climbed up on the table where he could reach the picture, and began marking around the child's sunny curls. Then he went to work on the lamb, and in a little while the meek-looking animal was changed into a curly tailed dog.

The cathedral bells pealed out the hour of noon, and mingling with them like golden-throated bird calls came the chimes from the Alcazar. But Bartolome did not hear. He

BARTOLOME'S VELVET HAT 91

was lost in his drawing, and when his mother opened the door he was still busily at work.

Maria Perez looked at him with horrified eyes, and then at the picture that had altered so in her absence. Instead of the boy and the lamb she had known from childhood, a lad in a cavalier's hat caressed a saucy-faced dog.

"Oh, Bartolome!" she exclaimed; "you have ruined it!"

But Bartolome turned in surprise. He was conscious of having done no harm.

"I am sure the boy will be happier now," he said, "because he has a hat and a dog."

But Maria Perez shook her head and seemed very unhappy, and when his father came home and found what he had done, he was locked up in the cellar. So instead of going out where the boys could see his new hat, and greeting his Aunt Eulalia when she arrived, he had to stay in darkness and disgrace.

Evening brought the Padre Pedro, the wisest man in all Seville, and the good friend and adviser of the family. He was surprised at not seeing Bartolome, for the boy loved him and often ran to meet him, and when told that he had been so bad they had to lock him up, he could hardly believe it. Black-eyed Bartolome, who was usually so good! It did not seem possible that he should need punishing so severely, and the old man wanted to know about it.

"Oh, good padre!" Maria Perez said with tears in her eyes; "he has ruined my 'Boy and the Lamb,' marked it all over with charcoal."

Padre Pedro lifted his brows in surprise. That was indeed a very serious offense.

"Marked it over with charcoal," he repeated. "I did not think Bartolome would do anything like that!"

They took him in to see, but when he stood in front of the picture a look came into his face that was very tender.

"The blessed boy!" he exclaimed. "He was so happy over his own hat that he wanted the child to have one like it. I thought he had scratched and defaced it. But he meant no harm, I am sure. Call him and let us see."

So Bartolome was brought from his place of prison to tell his story to the padre, and as

Memories of the moor

BARTOLOME'S VELVET HAT 95

he came he wondered if he too would say he had been very wicked.

"Why did you do it?" the old man asked.

"I wanted the boy to have a hat like mine," came the earnest reply. "And I was sure he'd like a dog better than a sheep, so I changed that too. I didn't mean to be bad, Padre Pedro. Truly I didn't."

"I know it," said the padre kindly. "And your father and mother know too."

Bartolome was not locked up again that evening, but stayed in the room where they planned about finding him a drawing master.

"A boy who can draw like that must have a teacher."

And because it was Padre Pedro who said it, and he was so very wise, his father and mother and aunt thought so too.

"We can place him with my uncle, Juan de Castillo," said Maria Perez, "for no one in Seville can teach better than he."

So Bartolome Murillo began to study art, and while he was still a boy painted two pictures that people said proved he would be great. His parents no longer grieved because he had tampered with the family picture, for Padre Pedro declared he would be glad to have it in his study. So there it hung for many years, even after the old priest was gone, and the figures were no longer clear, so that it looked just like a spotted piece of paper. And Murillo's paintings still hang in the world's great galleries, and the years have not faded them any more than they have dimmed the glory of his name. To this day it is the pride of Spain, and the people of Seville love to talk of his childhood there, and of the time when he was a pupil of Castillo, who, although he was considered a very wonderful painter in those days, is remembered now chiefly because he was the teacher of Murillo.

If you are ever in Spain, go to the old town in the South that is still rich in memories of the Moor. And perhaps, some evening when the brilliant southern sunset touches the stucco houses with rainbow tints, and great folk in the balconies sit listening to guitars in the street below tinkling a sweet accompaniment to feet flying in a fandango, if you love the place well enough to try to make friends with its sunny-hearted people,

BARTOLOME'S VELVET HAT

some stately old cavalier or soft-voiced dame may tell you, as only they of Seville can tell it, the story of Bartolome's Velvet Hat.

THE WHITTLER OF CREMONA

VI

THE WHITTLER OF CREMONA

IT was sundown and Maytime, and Cremona was gay in the wealth of green and gold weather. Revelers in fantastic attire went laughing along the promenades, for it was the last day of carnival week, and grave men and women had been transformed into merry-eyed maskers. Instead of a solemn clerk in office or shop there was a jolly shepherd, or perhaps a dryad, while money-lenders who on other days looked stern and forbidding frisked about as goats or clowns or apes. Yes, it was gay in Cremona, for it was May and carnival time, and they come but once a year.

Down in a narrow, alley-like street that crept, zigzag fashion, toward the Duomo, three boys were standing in the shadows. They wore no masks, not even a scarlet brow-shield to show that they had any part in the merriment that was general on the boulevards, and the shabbiness of their clothing told that they were of Cremona's poor. Perhaps they had crept from the bright-robed throng because of their somber attire; perhaps just to talk over a question that seemed important, for two of them were in earnest conversation, while the third stood quietly by, whittling at a pine stick. He was younger than the others, with a sensitive face and big, expressive eyes that were brown and velvety, and his companions called him Tonio.

"But I tell you, Salvator, every minute lost now is like throwing gold away. People are generous at carnival time, and we can get twenty lira to-night as easily as one when the fun is over, for a merry heart makes an open hand."

"Perhaps you are right, Gulio, and I will go. Shall we start now?"

His brother nodded and replied, "Yes, to the piazza, in front of the Duomo, where a crowd is always passing. You sing, and I will play. Do you want to go too, Tonio?"

Antonio looked up from the stick that was

THE WHITTLER OF CREMONA 103

beginning to take the semblance of a dagger under his knife, and turned his velvet eyes full on Gulio.

"Yes. I'd like to be with you, even if I cannot sing."

The brothers laughed.

"You certainly cannot sing," Gulio remarked. "You can do nothing but whittle, which is a pity, for that never turns a penny your way. But hurry. People are in their merriest mood now."

And laughing voices sounding from the streets told that he was right.

Gulio picked up his violin, and, followed by Salvator and Antonio, led the way through the alley to a street that skirted the Po. Other Cremonese, both old and young, moved in the same direction, for all wanted to be where the fun was at its height, and that was in the great square in front of the Duomo. The brothers chatted as they went along, for the thought of the money the revelers would give had made them light of heart. But Antonio said little. Gulio's remark that he could do nothing but whittle was still in his mind, and while he knew it to be true, it made him sad. He loved music, yet could have no part in making it, for he did not own a violin, and when he tried to sing his voice squeaked so that the boys laughed. It was hard to be just a whittler when his companions could play and sing well.

Soon they were in front of the great cathedral, where a throng continually moved by, the brilliancy of the masks and dominos seeming to vie with the hues nature had spread across the sky. For the sun had dropped like a ball of flame on the broad Lombardian plains beyond the city, and masses of purple and maroon clouds were piled along the horizon. Now and then a sail fluttered like a white-winged bird as a pleasure bark moved up or down the river, and gold-emblazoned standards and rich caparisons on the horses and carriages of great lords added color to the scene. There is a saying that all nature is glad when Cremona makes merry, and the glowing beauty of the evening seemed to prove it true.

Without losing a minute Gulio took his violin from its case, and tuning it with skilful fingers, began the prelude of a Lombardian folk song. Salvator's voice was sweet and lute-like, and as he sang to his brother's accompaniment, several stopped to listen, and dropped coins into the singer's outstretched hand when he finished.

Antonio kept on with his whittling until it was so dark he could not see to work. Then he sat on the cathedral steps and waited for the boys.

A man walked by. He wore neither mask nor domino, and seemed to care little about the gaiety. But seeing the youthful musicians, he came close to where they stood.

"That is a pretty song, lad," he said as Salvator finished another ballad. "Would you sing it again to please a lonely man's fancy?"

He seemed to hear nothing but the music as the boy did as he asked, and stood with half-closed eyes listening to the fresh young voice that blended sweetly with the soft violin accompaniment. Then, handing Salvator a coin, he went on down the street, without noticing Antonio, who still sat on the steps.

The boy held the coin up in the waning light and gave a cry.

"*Sacre giorno!*"[1] A gold piece! A gold piece for one song!"

Gulio looked at him dubiously. But when he examined the coin, he too exclaimed, "Truly a gold piece! But he can well afford it. That is the great Amati."

Antonio came and looked at the money. He had seen very few gold pieces, and thought it wonderful that a man should give so much. Then, turning to Gulio, he asked, "Who is Amati, and why do you call him great?"

Salvator stared in amazement.

"You have not heard of Amati?" he asked.

But before he could answer Gulio interrupted, "Of course not. Antonio is just a whittler. He knows about knives and woods, but little about music. Amati is a violin maker, the greatest in Italy, and very, very rich. Yet men say he cares for nothing in the world but his work."

The brothers were so happy over their good fortune that they were not willing to

---

[1] *Sacre giorno*—holy day.

Day after day he toiled in the workshop

THE WHITTLER OF CREMONA 109

stay in the street any longer. They wanted to get home with the money, and Antonio had no desire to be there alone. It is jolly to watch a throng of merry-makers when one has companions, but not pleasant to be in the midst of gaiety in which you have no part. So he walked with them as far as the bridge across the Po, then went on to his own home and crept to bed. But he did not sleep, for his brain was afire with a thought that had just come into it. He could not sing. He could do nothing but whittle, and here in his own Cremona was a man who with knives and wood made wonderful violins.

Before dawn next day he was up, and eating a piece of bread, took some things he had made with his knife, and crept out of the house while his parents were still sleeping. Somewhere in the city the master violinmaker dwelt, and he meant to find his home. It was not hard, for all Cremona knew of the great Amati, and while the matin bells were still ringing Antonio stood at his door.

The servant growled because he disturbed the house so early and scolded him away, so he waited in the street until he was sure it was time for work to begin, when again he rattled the heavy brass knocker. Again the man was about to drive him away, when the master, hearing the hireling's angry tones and the boy's pleading ones, came to the door.

"I have brought these things for you to see," Antonio answered when questioned. "I cut them out with my knife, and want to know if you think I can learn to make violins."

The great man smiled.

"What is your name, lad?"

"Antonio Stradivarius," came the eager reply.

"And why do you want to make violins?"

The boy's face was very earnest as he looked into the master's, and the velvet eyes seemed to grow darker as he spoke.

"Because I love music, and cannot make any. Salvator and Gulio can both sing and play. You heard them last night in the piazza in front of the Duomo and gave them the gold piece. I love music as much as they, but my voice is squeaky. I can do nothing but whittle."

THE WHITTLER OF CREMONA 111

The master laid his hand on Antonio's shoulder.

"Come into the house and you shall try. The song in the heart is all that matters, for there are many ways of making music. Some play violins, some sing, some paint pictures and make statues, while others till the soil and make flowers bloom. Each sings a song, and helps to make music for the world. If you put your best into it, the song you sing with knives and wood will be just as noble as the one Salvator and Gulio sing with voice or violin."

So Antonio Stradivarius, a boy who could not sing, became a pupil of the great Amati. Day after day he toiled in the workshop. Day after day he hewed persistently and patiently, until at last he had a violin. It was not done in a week, nor in a month, for the master taught him many lessons beside those in cutting and shaping and string placing, one of which was that a tiny bit well done each day is what means great achievement by and by. Sometimes he wanted to hurry and work less carefully than his teacher advised, but gradually he learned that patience is worth more than all things else to him who would excel, and when the instrument was finished he felt repaid for the long days of toil, for the master praised it, and that was a wonderful reward.

Years passed, and he worked on and on. His squeaky voice no longer troubled him, for although it had not improved, and Gulio and Salvator were both singers much loved in Cremona, he had learned that Amati's words were true, and that if there is a song in the heart there is always a way of singing it. So he put his best into his work, and his violins became known all over Italy. Musicians said their tone was marvelously sweet and mellow, and wondered how it could be. But to Antonio it seemed very simple, and he said it was just because he put so much love into the making.

At last Amati died and his pupil took his place as the master violin-maker of Italy. Salvator and Gulio's voices had become squeaky, and people no longer cared to hear them, but still Antonio kept steadily on at his much-loved work, trying to make each violin better and more beautiful than the one before it.

That was over two hundred years ago, and now, at the mention of Cremona, men think not of the fair city beside the Po whose stately Duomo still looks out over the fertile plains of Lombardy, but of the world's greatest violin-maker, Antonio Stradivarius. There is no civilized land into which his instruments have not been taken, for musicians prize them more highly than any others, and refuse for them sums greater than any of which the boy Antonio had ever heard. To own a "Strad" is to be rich indeed, and one of the things of which Italy is proudest is that it was the land of Antonio Stradivarius. All of which goes to show that although one can do nothing but whittle, he may help to make music for the world if there is a song in the heart, and a noble purpose and patience and persistence keep the hands at work.

A BIT O' PINK VERBENA

VII

A BIT O' PINK VERBENA

ONCE upon a time a many-gabled house stood in a quaint quarter of old Hamburg. It was a stately structure, and the people living there were rich and cultured. They had flocks and herds and merchant vessels and gold and silver plate, and their name was known to every one in the harbor town. But for all their possessions they were not honored as the wealthy usually are, for they were of the race of Israel, which in that day was scorned and shunned. But that mattered little to them. They were happy in their home beside the Elbe, and there, in the year of our Lord 1809, a child was born. The moon gleamed gloriously over the fresh-fallen snow on that eventful night, and a star, like an angel's eye, peeped through the half-open blind into the room where the baby lay. The old nurse said it was a good omen, and meant that he would be great and happy, so when the christening time came they named him Felix.

Twelve years passed, and the babe born in Hamburg had become a boy in Berlin. His home was a splendid house in the Neue Promenade, set in the heart of a lovely garden, and there was only one thing he liked better than to race through the grounds with his sister or to have tugs of war with his brothers. That was to work at his music—but that comes later in the story. He was slender and delicate looking for his years, but could run and leap and climb like an Indian.

One autumn morning when the martens were moving in long black lines away from Berlin, and now and then a weird cry above the tree tops told that a flock of storks was making its flight toward Egypt, there was a romp in the Mendelssohn garden. Felix was chief of a brigand band, and Fanny a captive girl the brothers were carrying away into the mountains. It was a favorite game with all of them, and they played it with a vim, until, just as the weeping victim was

A BIT O' PINK VERBENA 119

being thrust into a cave to be held for ransom, a maid called from the doorway.

"Come in, children," she said. "Your mother has a surprise for you."

Instantly the play stopped and there was a rush for the house. In the living-room they found a man talking with the mother, and at sight of him came exclamations and merry greetings. It was Herr Zelter, Felix's teacher and their good comrade, who always had a tale or a riddle, and was never too tired to entertain them. Fanny hurried to ask if he would n't tell her the answer to the last conundrum he gave, because, try as she would, she could not guess it.

Everybody laughed as he told it, and Fanny felt quite stupid for not having thought of it herself, and was sure the boys would tease her. But they did n't, because, before they had a chance, there came a wonderful message.

"Felix and I are going to take a vacation trip," Herr Zelter announced. "What think you of a journey through the Harz Mountains and into the provinces beyond?"

A shout went up from the brothers and sisters, but Felix stood silent for a moment and looked in big-eyed wonder.

"The Harz Mountains," he said as if awakened from a dream.

"Yes," the mother spoke gently. "Do you want to go?"

"Do I want to go?" he repeated. "Oh, mother, it will be splendid."

Frau Mendelssohn smiled. She was a beautiful woman, with velvet, lustrous eyes, and her face, like her voice, was sweet.

"I knew you would like it," she said as she stroked his soft, dark hair. "You have worked hard at your music and studies, and deserve a vacation."

And the brothers and sisters nodded as if they thought so too.

"Yes," Herr Zelter added, "and there may be some surprises along the way."

Felix was so excited over the prospect that he could n't eat his lunch, and Fanny declared he 'd get as thin as a fish worm. But the picture she painted of him did n't seem to make any difference, for although he usually had a healthy boy's appetite, he had none at all now, and could n't think of anything but

A BIT O' PINK VERBENA 121

wild mountain passes, and caves, and haunted glens. He had always wanted to go into the Harz country, for he had heard many fantastic tales of the elves and gnomes peasants say abound in that region and play pranks on all who come their way, but had no idea he would get there so soon. Sometimes, however, wishes come true. That very afternoon he and his teacher left Berlin, and then wonderful things came to pass.

Once in the highlands there was always something interesting and exciting. One day, as they followed the forest path up Mt. Kyffhäuser, a woodman pointed to a grotto where the country folk declare Frederick Barbarossa sleeps beside a banquet table. Felix listened, fascinated, to the mountain legend of how the emperor's beard had grown until it trails on the ground, and will continue to grow for ages and ages, until it has wound seven times around the legs of the table. Then the monarch will awaken, bestride a charger, and scatter his foes, after which time there will be peace as long as the world lasts. He was wild to get inside the cavern, but the peasant shook his head and said it was impossible. Only once a twelve-month, when the cock crows with the dawning of the new year, can the enchanted grotto open, and woe to him who tries to force an entrance at any other time! So he knew it was useless to coax, but made up his mind to came back some New Year's Eve. Then they went to a miners' carnival and joined in the yearly festivities of the salt seekers, after which there was a visit to a clock making village. One delight followed another as they journeyed, until at last they came to Weimar.

Felix was up at dawn the next morning, for they had been stopping only one day in each place, and he wanted to see as much as possible of this one. He went with Gretchen, the inn maid, when she drove the geese to pasture, and she told him many things about her native town.

"There is the castle where the Grand Duke lives," she said, pointing to a great structure whose towers rose above the frost-painted maples; "and beyond is the cathedral with the chimes."

Felix nodded.

A BIT O' PINK VERBENA 123

"Yes," he answered, "Herr Zelter told me about them. I think Weimar is a wonderful place, because Goethe lives here."

"Ah, yes," the girl said softly, "the master! Are n't you glad you are going to see him?"

Felix whirled and looked at her.

"Going to see him!" he exclaimed; "what makes you say that?"

Gretchen twisted her yellow braids into a rope and smiled as she answered, "Because I heard Herr Zelter tell Frau Lippe last evening that you came to Weimar to visit Goethe."

Felix did n't want to hear another word. He turned and ran from the grazing place along the path that led back to the inn, and people who saw him wondered why he hurried so. Over rock heaps and brambles he bounded with long, agile leaps, and did not stop until he came to the stone stairway leading up to the entrance of Elephant Inn.

Herr Zelter stood on the topmost step watching him, and at sight of him the boy gave a joyous exclamation.

"Is it true?" he cried as he dashed up the

steps. "Gretchen says we are going to visit Herr Goethe."

His teacher smiled and answered, "Yes, that is why I brought you to Weimar. Did n't I tell you in Berlin that there might be a surprise?"

"In Berlin," Felix repeated. "Did you know it there?"

"To be sure I did. The master wrote me, asking that I bring you because he wants to hear you play. That is why we started on the trip, and because you are so fond of surprises, your mother and I decided to keep it a secret, so you would enjoy it even more."

Felix could hardly believe what he heard. It seemed impossible the great Goethe could have sent for him, not because he was accustomed to being shunned because he was a Hebrew boy, for he never had been made unhappy by that. There was more refinement and better understanding in the Prussian capital than in the harbor town, and the culture and sterling qualities of the Mendelssohns won them the friendship of Jew and Gentile alike. But Goethe was the master poet of Germany, to whom even princes gave

A BIT O' PINK VERBENA 125

homage, and why should he care about the playing of a little Berlin boy? All of which goes to show what an unspoiled, lovable lad Felix was.

He stood wondering about it until Herr Zelter said, "Go and make yourself presentable, for we start in half an hour."

It was not necessary to tell him a second time. He ran upstairs and changed his clothes so rapidly that long before the half hour was over he was waiting for Herr Zelter in the hall.

Just as they started, Gretchen, the inn maid, came running after them, waving a cluster of pink blossoms.

"Here," she called as Felix turned toward her. "Give these to the master. Frau Lippe let me take them from the house box, and there are no lovelier ones in Weimar."

And she handed him a cluster of verbena, each petal of which was perfectly unfolded and pink as the heart of a conch shell.

Felix never forgot that walk as he and Zelter went along the maple-skirted promenade toward the home of Goethe, never forgot the splendid houses of the great, the ducal palace, the cathedral, the peasant cottages, and the wind-whipped fields they passed on the way, and years afterward described them as vividly as if they had been beheld only a half hour before, for every sight in Weimar seemed to be painted on his brain in unfading colors. He walked eagerly, expectantly beside his teacher, and finally they came to a great house, rambling like a Saxon citadel, and heavily windowed on every side. As they went in at the gate a voice from among the trees called, "Zelter! Have you brought the Mendelssohn boy from Berlin?"

A heavy, rather short man, with blue, piercing eyes and hair softly flecked with gray, came down the path to meet them. Then Felix heard his teacher saying, "This is Herr Goethe," and he knew he was face to face with the poet all Germany declared was greater than a king.

Impulsively he took the wrinkled hand outstretched to meet his own, and presented the verbena Gretchen gave him. His blue eyes were luminous as the master smiled down on the blossoms, saying, "Thank you, boy, and

A BIT O' PINK VERBENA 127

thank the little inn maid too. I shall keep them and remember you both."

Suddenly, from the cathedral tower, came the notes of an old German choral, and a Kyrie Eleison, sweet as an angel's song, sounded across the garden. Felix stood like one entranced, drinking in the beauty of the music and forgetting everything but the glory of the chimes. Perhaps he would have stayed there for a long time in a sort of revery, but the master, who had been watching him curiously, laid his hand on his shoulder and said, "Let us go into the house now, for I want to hear music sweeter than that of the chimes."

Then Felix remembered what Herr Zelter had told him, and wondered if the men could hear his heart beating. It seemed they must, for joy had set it thumping like a hammer, because he knew the master meant to ask him to play.

Half an hour later the drawing-room of the Goethe house was flooded with light. The master and Frau Goethe, Fräulein Ulrike, her sister, Herr Zelter, the Schopenhauers, and several other friends sat side by side. But no one spoke. No one thought of anything or heard anything but exquisite music exquisitely rendered. Was it an angel orchestra dispensing such sweet sounds? No, it came from the piano at the touch of a brown-haired boy. Little wonder they seemed bound by enchantment as they listened. Little wonder smiles and tears played hide-and-seek in the poet's eyes, for Felix Mendelssohn Bartholody, then just turned thirteen, was playing a fugue from Bach.

He finished, and Goethe went over and laid his hand on the dark head.

"You have given me an hour of pleasure," he said tenderly. "What can I do to reward you?"

Felix looked at him, as if wondering what to request. Then a smile flashed across his face and he spoke in a low voice, "Sire, I should be glad if you would give me a kiss."

And the gray-haired immortal bent and kissed the brow of him who was destined to become an immortal, while Zelter and the others applauded, and bonny Adele Schopen-

A BIT O' PINK VERBENA 129

hauer set a wreath of leaves on the brown head.

"To crown you, like a victor!" she exclaimed.

And the next day Felix wrote home to his mother in Berlin, "After that we all had supper together, and I sat on the master's right. Now, every morning, I have a kiss from the author of 'Faust' and 'Werther,' and two kisses from friend and father Goethe. Think of that!"

Just at dawn several mornings later Zelter shook Felix out of a sleep.

" Get up quickly!" he exclaimed. "Don't you remember that to-day the Grand Duke and Duchess and the hereditary Grand Duke are coming to visit? Bestir yourself, and don't lie there as if nothing extraordinary is about to happen."

The lad looked up, blinking, for he was just like other boys, and not eager to get out of bed in the morning.

"Y-yes," he muttered, "but that is n't as wonderful as being here alone with Goethe. Mother says no one, not even a king, is as great as he."

And Zelter nodded agreement, for he, too, believed that. But he hurried the boy out of bed and into his clothes, and soon afterward the royal visitors arrived.

Of course they wanted to hear Felix play, for they had been told of the concert that ended with a fugue from Bach, but even if they had known nothing about it they would have been eager to listen to his music, for Felix Mendelssohn Bartholody, even at that time, was known throughout Germany as a wonder child. Great folk in Berlin, as well as strangers who visited the Prussian capital, delighted in going to his home in the Neue Promenade, for Abraham and Leah Mendelssohn, his father and mother, were among the brilliant scholars of their day. The charm of their conversation was a magnet to draw the gifted, and their reception hall became one of the noted German salons. Painters, musicians, scholars, learned men, and beautiful women gathered there, and whenever guests came Felix played, sometimes alone, sometimes in duet with his sister Fanny, and always his hearers wondered if it was really a child who made such lovely

A BIT O' PINK VERBENA 131

music. They took word of his attainments to their homes and their friends, and although he never had appeared in public, the story of the Hebrew prodigy spread. Thus Goethe heard of his genius, and became so interested in the lad that he asked Zelter to bring him to Weimar. So of course the Grand Duke and Duchess would have wanted to hear him, even if they had known nothing of that memorable Sunday night.

Well, Felix played. He began at eleven in the morning, and finished at ten that night, stopping to rest only two hours during that long period. The royal visitors were delighted, and said such charming things about his genius that he'd have had his head turned if he had not been a very sensible boy. But he had a wonderful mother, and praise from the royal family did not mean half as much to him as praise from the poet meant. He was glad he had pleased them, for they were pleasant and kind, but most of all he was glad he had pleased Goethe.

The days passed joyously, with games and sports in the garden and quiet hours at the piano, with the poet sitting close by listening while he played. These were times of rare delight to Felix.

"Every afternoon," he wrote home to his mother, "he opens the piano and says, 'Now make a little noise for me.' And that voice of his! Mother, the sound of it is wonderful. He can shout like ten thousand warriors, yet when he speaks tc me it seems very soft and low."

Gladly he would have stayed on in Weimar for weeks and months, but that could not be. A fortnight after his arrival he went home with Zelter, bearing with him recollections of a never-to-be-forgotten visit, and leaving behind with the poet memories that were sweet.

Then swiftly sped the days, and wonderful triumphs they brought to Felix Mendelssohn Bartholody. He began playing in public, at concerts and musicfests of the Prussian capital, and people went by thousands to see the boy and listen to his music, to have a good look at the lad who was the pet and favorite of Goethe. And how he played at those memorable concerts, sometimes difficult numbers from the masters, sometimes melodies of

A BIT O' PINK VERBENA 133

his own composing, always with feeling, always with exquisite finish, and always with light divine in his gleaming eyes.

Then, between public appearances, there were joyful days at home with his sister Fanny in the Garden House, a place as beautiful and sweet as could be imagined. A fountain plashed by the window, and all summer long birds held concert in the linden boughs. Here together brother and sister read Shakespeare's "Midsummer Night's Dream," and here, when seventeen, Felix composed the music suggested by that fairy play, which, had he never created another melody, would have made his name immortal.

After that, other works followed in rapid succession. He loved his music and kept at it constantly, resting occasionally by taking a trip into some quaint nook of Germany, traveling on foot in the vagabond way. Then he would return to work, composing every day, with Fanny, his gifted sister, and his mother, who were his first and best teachers, auditors and critics. If they pronounced a work good he was satisfied, and no taunts from envious but less gifted musicians could shake his faith in the worth of a composition when it had been secured by the approval of those at home.

Thus Felix Mendelssohn Bartholody, at an age when most boys are thinking of beginning their life-work, was secure and famous in his. England called him, and France and Austria, and honors innumerable were heaped upon him. But they did not shrivel and warp his soul. He was the child of Leah Mendelssohn, that rare, gentle woman whose fragrant nature and brilliant intellect would have made her home the retreat of the great of Berlin even if it had not housed a wonder child, and he never forgot the lessons learned during those early days. His nature was as lovable as his genius was great, and the beggar in the streets, the child in the market place, rich, poor, and mighty alike, received a pleasant word and kindly smile from him. The brown hair Goethe loved had turned black now, but his eyes were as blue and tender, his soul was as sweet and serene as in those distant Weimar days.

Like Mozart and Chopin, this great master died early, before he was forty-five, yet in his short career enriching the world as much as if he had lived through many lifetimes, for his soul was pure, his heart was kind, and his genius was supreme. Goethe loved him in childhood, Germany adored him in manhood, and the world reveres his memory now that his work is done. It is sweet to think that the great are always simple, unassuming as little children, tender of memories, loyal to friends, gentle and compassionate toward the unfortunate. This was Felix Mendelssohn Bartholody, the child of Leah. He never forgot those Weimar days, never ceased to think of the great poet as "friend and father Goethe." How do we know? Because after he went to his rest, they found among his treasured things a bunch of dead stuff that once had been a nosegay, blackened and withered to the color of earth, and seeming as if it never could have been a cluster of blossoms. It was the verbena cut from the window box by the golden-haired inn maid and given by Felix to the author of "Faust." Upon the death of the poet it was returned to the musician, who treasured it with memories of those fragrant days, and for years it remained among the Mendelssohn relics, a memorial of the day when two of the world's immortals, one gray and crowned with the laurels of achievement, the other with his childhood still about him, stood in a garden at Weimar, while November winds whistled through the trees, and cathedral bells chimed out a Kyrie Eleison.

And what of the Hamburgers who had scorned his people because they were of the race of Israel? They seemed to have forgotten that, or to have grown ashamed of it, and were proud indeed of the fact that Felix was born among them. They spoke fondly of "unser Mendelssohn," and never in the history of the harbor town was there such a storm of indignation as when some of the people of Prussia tried to make it appear that he was a native of Berlin.

"No, he is ours," declared their northern neighbors, "for he was born among us."

And so these great capitals disputed and contended for the honor of having cradled a Hebrew baby, just as, long, long ago, seven Grecian cities each claimed to have been the birthplace of a blind old man.

A SHEPHERD LAD OF TUSCANY

VIII

A SHEPHERD LAD OF TUSCANY

APRIL had come, bringing flower and bird weather to the sweet Italian land of Tuscany, and even along the Apennine slopes, where the blossom carpet was not so heavy as in the sunny lowlands, buttercups and wild daffodils made golden rugs beneath the ilex-trees. They stretched away in shining patches to the vine-draped Fiesole hills, from which other rugs of gayer bloom and richer verdure sloped down to the silver Arno. Blue skies above, bird song and blossom breath sweetening the air, it was surely a time for merrymaking and joyous words. Yet two boys in charge of a flock on the hills above Vespignano looked at each other with excited faces, and the older one spoke so angrily to his companion that the lad winced as if struck.

"You have so little courage that even if you go, you won't amount to anything. So stay here, because you're not brave enough to try the world!"

The dark eyes of the younger were wide with hurt surprise.

"Do you mean that you think me a coward, Pasquali?" he asked, his sensitive lips quivering as if it required an effort to keep back the tears.

Pasquali shrugged his shoulders. He was fond of Giotto, and had not meant to grieve him, yet he felt provoked because he did not agree to his plan.

"Not exactly that," he replied more gently. "But can't you see that, as long as we stay here in Vespignano, we must go on herding sheep, while yonder in the city there is a chance of becoming rich?"

And as he spoke he pointed down to where Florence lay in her valley beside the Arno, all white and gold against the blue of the Lucca mountains, like a bit of fairy-land.

"It is beautiful there, Giotto," he urged, "with marble palaces instead of peasant huts, and the people wear fine clothes, and are happy. Come along, and be something bigger than a shepherd."

SHEPHERD LAD OF TUSCANY 141

For a minute, Giotto's face was afire with anticipation. He knew that Cimabue, the greatest of Italian painters, would come soon to decorate the castello, and that the count was sending men to the city next day to be his escort. For weeks, Pasquali had been urging him to run away and join the cavalcade beyond Fiesole, from which point they could travel along together, and, as members of the noble's train, gain admission to Florence, which would not be possible for two boys alone. Pasquali had a golden flow of words, and so dazzling was his picture of the luxurious life they might lead there, that Giotto was almost persuaded. But it was only for a minute. Then he shook his head, and answered: "No, Father needs me here. Besides, I have no money, and even if it does seem cowardly, I am afraid to go to the city without even a lira."

Pasquali laughed, not pleasantly but with a sneer, as if to mock the fears of his companion. He was two years older, and so large and strong that he looked like a man. Little he hesitated about leaving Vespignano, and was so confident of his ability to make his way anywhere that he pressed his timid friend with promises to look out for him.

"You can send money home to your father, and even if it is a little hard at first, anything will be better than this lonely life of herding."

But as Giotto looked at the white-fleeced sheep around him, and then at the village below, he thought differently. He saw his grandfather, too old to follow a herd now, laughing with some of the children, as if all the world were glad, and his sister Teresa, dark-eyed and graceful, go singing into the hut where his grandmother sat spinning. Just beyond, white-haired Armando, bent and feeble too, hobbled along on his stick, beckoning and smiling to those who hailed him as he passed, while gay young Serafino, who had broken a leg a fortnight before while rescuing a lamb from a precipice, was taking the sun and trying to gain strength to go back to his flock. Shepherd folk all were they, and there were no merrier hearts in Tuscany. So if those could be happy who had never seen the city except as they looked down on its gleaming towers from the hills

SHEPHERD LAD OF TUSCANY 143

where they pastured their flocks, it did n't seem a bad life after all. The ilex-tufted slopes that Pasquali was so eager to leave were home to Giotto. He was born in a hut below, and, as far back as his memory went, could look out of its northern window on the Apennines. And there had always been the music of the Mugone stream, now yellow and muddy, now shimmering like a silver ribbon flung down from the peaks, as it hurried away to join the Arno. Pasquali was an orphan, and had lived in many places, one of which was as dear as another. But to the boy who had never been beyond the grazing lands, there was only one home spot, and that was in Vespignano. Why, then, should he leave it for a place where he would be friendless and might perhaps have to go hungry? And that question he put to Pasquali.

"Besides," he continued, "herding does n't seem so dreadful. I love my sheep, and often when the hours seem long I make pictures in the sand. Then I forget that I am lonely."

Pasquali sneered. "Stay on and be a

shepherd if you think the life so fine. But look out that the count never catches you drawing when you are out with the sheep, for he will tell your father, and then there will be trouble. But I mean to be a great man, and do something finer than follow a flock."

And he strode away before Giotto could tell him that once, when he was drawing, the count had come by, and, instead of making trouble, had seemed much interested.

Pasquali kept his word and went away that night, and, in the days that followed, Giotto wondered much about him, hoping he would be successful in the city. Of course no word came back, for at that time letters had to go by courier, which cost so much that only the rich sent messages, while the poor had to be satisfied with wondering and hoping. He did not doubt that the lad would be able to make his way, for he was so big and strong that of course people would give him work, and Giotto even planned for the time when he might appeal to him.

"When I am older and can earn more," he mused, "I will go and ask Pasquali to help

SHEPHERD LAD OF TUSCANY 145

me find work; for, if I send a few lire home each week, it will not be hard for Father."

For little did he dream that a time would come when he would not need Pasquali's aid, and that Florence would be as proud of him as of her most illustrious prince.

Several days later, as he ate his lunch on the hillside, he heard the blare of trumpets announcing the arrival of Cimabue the painter, and saw the train go up to the castle gate. The splendidly groomed horses held their plumed heads high, while gold and silver mountings on saddle and bridle made them seem like fairy steeds. Banners and pennants floated, and brighter even than the scarlet coats of the attendants was the artist's crimson mantle; and, as the solitary lad watched the gorgeous cavalcade go into the courtyard and out of sight, he thought that to be a painter must be better than to be a prince. Then, taking up a piece of slate he had found that morning, he began making pictures of his sheep.

Everything else went out of his mind. He forgot that he was a peasant and lived in a poor hut, forgot everything in his love of sketching, and, as soon as one picture was finished, he rubbed it out and made another. Sometimes a lamb came up, caressing him with its velvet nose, or a soft-eyed ewe lay down at his feet. But he did not know it, nor did he hear hoofs advancing from behind, or see two riders alight from their mounts. He was still lost in his drawing when a voice said, "This is the shepherd lad of whom I told you, the one who makes pictures in the sand."

Giotto jumped in alarm. He knew it was the count who spoke, and feared that he would be angry because he had not greeted him as the low-born should those of rank. But the nobleman was not displeased, for he thought of something finer than social distinction, and, taking the slate from the weather-browned hand, he gave it to his companion.

"See, Cimabue!" he said. "This is how he passes his lonely hours."

Giotto caught the name and it thrilled him. Cimabue! The king of Italian painters! He would laugh at such poor sketching.

SHEPHERD LAD OF TUSCANY 147

"Oh, sire, it is not worth looking at!" he exclaimed. "I did it just to keep from being lonely."

But Giovanni Cimabue did look at the slate, and, as he examined it, spoke some words to the count that the boy did not understand. Then he asked, "Would you like to be a painter?"

"A painter!" Giotto repeated. "Oh, yes, sire. But that is impossible, for Father is poor, and I must tend sheep."

"Opportunities come to those who deserve them," the great man replied, "and there is something for you beside a shepherd's life."

Then the two rode away, and, as they went, Giotto wondered what Cimabue meant. But he had not very long to wonder, for that same night they came to the peasant hut to ask that he might study painting. The decorations at the castle would require some weeks, and when the artist returned to Florence he would take the lad into his workshop. At first it seemed impossible that such a lovely thing could come to a herd boy, but when his father gave his word, and thanked both count and painter, he wondered what

Pasquali would think, Pasquali, who had taunted him with being too much of a coward to try his fortune in the city.

Giotto did not lead his sheep to the slopes next day, nor any day thereafter. But all through the golden summer, when around Fiesole were billows of many-colored bloom, and his own hills of Vespignano were painted with orange and russet, he worked with Cimabue at the castle. Every morning, when the sunrise tints still hung like flaming poppies along the peaks, he went from the hut in the village, and he came back again at night to dream of his brushes and colors. The count let one of his own shepherds tend the Bondone flock, so his studies brought no hardship to his people, and, as all the villagers loved him, so all were glad that he was to be a painter.

Meanwhile, in fair Florence, Pasquali was learning that the city is a monster waiting to devour those who approach her friendless and empty-handed. Day after day he tramped the streets from one shop to another, and up to doors of great houses where many servants were employed, looking for work,

Then Giotto went to the city

SHEPHERD LAD OF TUSCANY 151

and always he was met with the question, "What can you do?"

"In Vespignano I was a shepherd," he would reply; "but the life was dull, so I came away."

"Better go back," those disposed to be kind would say. "The city is no place for country lads." While others drove him away with angry words.

For weeks he slept under the sky and ate the bread of charity. Then, sick and discouraged, he started back to Vespignano.

Giotto, on his way home from the castle one evening, saw the weary, foot-sore lad go toward the hut that had once been his home, and wondered if it could be Pasquali, who had been so eager to get away. Hunger had made hollows in his cheeks, and only the soft, dark eyes, and the hair curling about the brow in the old way made him sure it was his friend.

"Pasquali *mio*," he called, falling into the tender speech of the old shepherd days; "why are you back? Did n't you like the city?"

"The city!" the boy repeated in horror.

"It is a black hole of misery to those without money. It were better had I stayed here with the sheep, because now perhaps I cannot get any sheep to tend."

Giotto forgot that the boy had scorned him for not being brave enough to try the world. He thought only that his friend was troubled, and that he wanted to help him.

"I am sure you can," he comforted. "Come home with me to-night, and to-morrow I will ask the count to give you work."

So the two went together to the hut, where the shepherd fare seemed good indeed to the discouraged lad; and the next day, although he had all the help he really needed, the count pitied the runaway and took him back.

The frosts came, and the chestnut-trees on the slopes wore coats of bronze. The walls of the castello had been beautified until nothing was left to be done, and the painter prepared to leave Vespignano. Then Giotto went to the city, the same Florence in which Pasquali had urged him to seek his fortune in the spring. But he did not steal away like a thief in the night. He went instead as one who departs with honor. All the shepherds

SHEPHERD LAD OF TUSCANY 153

of the valley met to say good-by, and the count himself, and Cimabue, the painter, rode beside him. No knight faring forth to conquest ever rode with higher hopes in his breast, and few have gone to greater honors. Hard work awaited him in the studio of the master, for Cimabue was an exacting teacher, and knew that, no matter how gifted, one does not excel except by painstaking, persistent effort of both hand and brain. But he was an appreciative teacher as well, and nothing pleased him as much as some new evidence of genius in the boy in whom he had such great faith.

Once he went away from the workshop, leaving Giotto busy there. The boy kept to his painting for a while, then, stopping to look at the half-finished work of his master, a mischievous idea possessed him. Seizing a brush, he painted a fly on the nose of the figure on the canvas, and so lifelike was his portrayal, that, when Cimabue returned, he tried to brush it away with his hand, before he discovered the trick his pupil had played on him. Yet he was not angry, for it was but another proof that the boy kept his eyes open and studied everything around him, without doing which no one can hope to be a painter.

Years passed, and Florence became a fairer and more glorious city because a peasant lad from the northern hills had taken up his abode there. He became an architect as well as a painter, and, whenever a new palace was to be builded or an old one needed beautifying, it was Giotto who was chosen for the work, because no one in Italy wrought such wonders as he. The lords of the land called him from one city to another. Naples, Pisa, Ravenna, Assisi, and even imperial Rome, clamored for a show of his genius; and, whenever he gave his time to a piece of work, it was as if a fairy hand had touched it.

But in Florence his heart seemed to rest, and there he put forth his noblest effort. Those who followed strove to make their work as fine as his, so the city of the Arno came to be a place of wonderful achievement.

The story of its loveliness has spread to every land, and to-day it is the treasure-house of Italy, possessing an untold wealth of art

SHEPHERD LAD OF TUSCANY 155

and some of the noblest buildings in the world, the most wonderful among them having been glorified by the hand of Giotto.

"Giotto's Campanile," men still call the matchless bell-tower that rises beside the Duomo. But of the thousands who go there to see it, only a few know that he who planned and partly built it was once a shepherd whom Cimabue found drawing on a piece of slate as he tended his flocks on the hills of Tuscany.

THE BORDER WONDERFUL

IX

THE BORDER WONDERFUL

IN the workshop of Josefo the goldsmith, black-eyed Andrea was assorting the tools. There was no one to talk to, and he did n't like the task a bit. He wanted to be out in the sunshine among the pomegranates and purple-starred myrtles, where he knew Beatrice was waiting for the procession, for he was only seven years old, and this would be the gayest carnival time of all the year. But boys in his day began their life-work very early, and it was already several months since he had been apprenticed to a goldsmith, who believed not at all that one should romp when a trade was to be learned. So there was nothing for him to do but group hammers and knives and chisels, and try to be content with seeing the parade go by.

Would Beatrice forget to signal him, he

wondered, with an anxious glance toward the window. Surely not, for she had promised to sing as soon as she saw the outriders. And just then a clear, sweet voice rose in a Florentine greeting song. Yes, it was coming now, the great cavalcade of which people had talked for many days, and he turned from the bench and hurried out into the loggia.

Leaning far out over the railing, he saw her standing under the pomegranates.

"Are they coming, Bice?" he asked, as her merry eyes turned toward him.

"*Si, si,* Andrea *mio,*" she called back in her musical Tuscan. "Yonder is the advance-guard, and just behind are the gleaming Medici banners. That means the ducal carriage will soon be here. Ah, it is splendid, splendid!"

And she whirled in a dancing step and broke into song again.

Andrea ran down the stairway, forgetting all about his task in the workshop. Yes, there it came, a gorgeous procession, across the Arno by the Ponte Vecchio and along the Via Guicciardini, horsemen and footmen in fine array, bearing Florence's duke to Florence's great cathedral. His birthday it was, and the people would celebrate it magnificently, Andrea knew, for his father, the jolly tailor, had told him all about it as he bent over his sewing the night before. There would be pomp at the palace and mirth in the streets, and he wished he might roam at will and feast upon it. But suddenly a harsh voice struck his ear, for the goldsmith had come into the shop and found him away.

"Get to your bench, young dullard, and quickly too!" he called. "A nice lot of trouble you make for me with your heedless ways, and I've a mind to send you back to your father."

And looking up at the face framed in the window, the boy saw that the eyes were as angry as the voice.

He was very much frightened. Twice that morning he had been scolded for drawing pictures when he should have been turning the tool grinder, and he wondered what dreadful thing would happen now. So he hurried in through the loggia to his bench; but his lip quivered as Beatrice went on with the crowd, and he thought how hard it would be to stay in the workshop when all the mirth and life of Florence was pulsing in the streets, and tears came so thick and fast that he could hardly tell one tool from another. Then the master went out, and Leonardo, the journeyman, returned from an errand. He was older than Andrea, but they were very good friends, and the doleful face brightened as he came near.

"What's the matter?" he asked, at the sight of the misty eyes. "Would n't he let you see the procession?"

The lad shook his head.

"No; he says I am here to work."

"Too bad, too bad," the older boy murmured. "But there will be other festivals, and he is n't often cross like this. He's worried now because he can't get a design for the border on the cardinal's bowl, for, unless it is finished this week there will be no more work from this great man. So it is not strange that he's out of sorts."

Andrea had no idea what a design was, and was too unhappy to care. His mind was on the merriment, and nothing seemed

THE BORDER WONDERFUL 163

half as bad as having to miss it. But he had to work. So he tried to make the best of it, and his hands moved so rapidly about the bench that soon his task was finished, and he had nothing to do until the master came in and assigned him to another. Leonardo, polishing a plate at his own place, was too busy to talk. So he took a piece of parchment and a bit of charcoal from the table and began to draw.

That made him forget his disappointment. He scratched and scratched on the smooth white surface, and by the time the journeyman had finished his polishing, the sheet was almost covered, and he held it up for him to see.

Leonardo looked, then gave an exclamation.

"Oh, oh! It is a pretty thing you have made, but you 've used some of the master's parchment, and he will be angry indeed."

For parchment was costly in those far-off days, and men were very careful of it.

Andrea was terrified, and, at the sight of Josefo coming in at the door, he began to cry.

"What have you been doing now?" the man asked angrily.

"This," he sobbed, laying his hand on the parchment.

Leonardo held his breath, for he was sure that Andrea, who so often irritated the master by his thoughtless ways, would fare badly at his hands. But as the goldsmith looked at the drawing the sternness left his face, and a sort of wonder came into it.

"You don't mean you did this?" he said.

"Yes," Andrea faltered, "but I 'm sorry I spoiled the parchment."

Then, as Josefo laid his big hand on the dark head, Leonardo wondered why he had ever thought him stern.

"Never fear about that," he replied, in a voice they seldom heard in the workshop. "You have done a wonderful thing, and it means much to me. I shall use this border for the cardinal's bowl, and to-morrow, when Gian Barile comes, I 'll show it to him. This afternoon you may have a holiday, for you deserve to see the fun for helping me out of my trouble."

And Andrea wondered how it happened

THE BORDER WONDERFUL 165

that the very thing that had brought him scoldings twice that morning should give him a merry time a few hours later. But he was only seven years old, and too young to realize what a wonderful thing he had done. But this he *did* know: he was going to have a great deal of pleasure. And beside the carnival fun there was the joy of looking forward to the morrow, when Gian Barile would see his drawing, for he was said by Florentines to be a most excellent painter.

Morning in the *bottéga* of the goldsmith was a very busy time. Tools must be ground, and knives sharpened, and metal prepared for the melting-pot. Then, too, chiseling and shaping and carving began on new articles, and there was always finishing on those left over from the day before. So Andrea and Leonardo worked busily, while the master carved away at the bowl. They talked and laughed as they bent to their tasks, for now that he had a design that suited him, Josefo was in a jolly mood, and when Beatrice, the gay street-singer, put her head in at the window, he did not scold, but called to her in a merry jest. Together they chatted about yesterday's carnival, and after a while came Gian Barile, to lounge and gossip for an hour.

Andrea saw him saunter up the via, and as he came in through the loggia whispered to Leonardo, "Do you think he will really show him my drawing?"

And even as they held their heads together, Josefo unrolled the parchment.

"What think you of this for the work of a lad?" he asked, as Barile appeared at the door.

The painter shook his head.

"No lad did that. Or, if it be really true, let me see him, and I will show you another Giotto or Tiziano or perhaps a Leonardo."

And Leonardo the journeyman jumped so that he dropped one of the costliest tools, which would have brought a stern rebuke at any other time. But the master did not notice it. His mind was upon other things.

"Aye, aye," he insisted, "upon the word of an honest Florentine it *is* the work of a lad, and he but a seven-year-old; young Andrea, the tailor's son."

"Upon the word of an honest Florentine it *is* the work of a lad"

THE BORDER WONDERFUL 169

For a minute Barile did not speak. Perhaps he was silent over the marvel of what the boy had done. Perhaps he thought of how he might aid him. He just stood and looked into the dark eyes, then said slowly, "If you will study faithfully, there will come a day when you will paint more gloriously than I can ever hope to."

And Andrea believed he must have heard wrong, for Barile was one of the celebrated artists of his time.

Then a thought troubled him.

Perhaps his father would not let him do it. He had been eager to have him become a goldsmith, and might think he could not be an artist. So Barile went home with him that night, and as they talked it over, the tailor said his advice seemed good, and he would let his boy follow it.

Which delighted Andrea so much that he ran as fast as he could to the pomegranate-shaded house where Beatrice lived, to tell her he was going to be a painter.

"That will be splendid!" she cried, as she clapped her sun-browned hands; "and when you are great, I will come and sing for you."

And they laughed together, thinking how fine it would be.

So, soon after he began his apprenticeship to the goldsmith, Andrea left it to work with brushes and pigments. He was a studious and faithful pupil, and progressed so rapidly that Barile soon realized he needed a better master, and spoke concerning him to Piero di Cosimo, the most renowned teacher of Florence, who agreed to take him under his care. Then came years of work, hard, unceasing, but happy work, for Andrea loved his brushes and canvases, and Cosimo loved his pupil, until he became so skilful with pigments that people said it seemed as if he had used them for half a century. Nothing delighted him as much as to blend his precious colors, and, while other lads loitered in the streets or roamed along the Arno, he painted in the shop of Cosimo, improving hour by hour and day by day, until all of Barile's prophecies concerning him were fulfilled, and Florence gloried in the thought of having produced another immortal.

So it was n't bad, after all, that he had to

THE BORDER WONDERFUL 171

stay in the workshop that carnival morn, for, although it seemed a hardship then, it brought him to the notice of Gian Barile, and the world came to have one more master painter. Almost four centuries have gone since he lived and worked, but artists still marvel at the beauty of his pictures, and strive, but always unsuccessfully, to copy their exquisite design and hue. Beatrice, singing away the hours under the pomegranates or along the sun-kissed vias, thought him a foolish boy for working so hard, for she could not understand that it was a divine thing that kept him at his pigments and would make him live forever.

And what became of the border he drew on parchment in the old *bottéga?* No one knows. Perhaps Josefo treasured it throughout his lifetime. Perhaps he sold it or gave it away. But that cannot be proven, because nothing is known of Josefo. His very name would have been forgotten long ago, had it not happened that once, for a very short time, he had an apprentice boy who gave him a deal of trouble drawing pictures when he should have been assorting tools.

But what then seemed wasted hours have proven to be hours well spent, for the lad grew to be an honor to his city and a glory to his land. And to this day, because he was the child of a maker of garments, he, like Tintoretto, the Venetian dyer's son, is still designated by his father's craft, and is known to the world as Andrea del Sarto.

THE WONDER-CHILD OF WARSAW

X

THE WONDER-CHILD OF WARSAW

THEY said he was nine years old, but he was so little and delicate looking that he seemed not a day over seven; and when the great Niemcewicz, a famous Polish writer, saw him standing in the doorway, watching the snow float down like fairy rose leaves, he was sure he had made a mistake and looked again at the address on the paper. But there it was, plain as ever an address was written; and since this was the street and number, of course this must be the boy. Yet how could it be—the sensitive-faced, fragile child, with his shock of curly hair and wide dark eyes that gleamed like living jewels—how could he be the lad of whom such wonderful tales were told in Warsaw?

And for a minute he just stood and wondered. And while he wondered, Frédéric wondered too, but about something very different from what was in the mind of the poet. Who was this velvet-coated stranger who rode in a carriage with a coat of arms and wore a crimson-plumed bonnet fine enough for a king? Great folk did not often come to his home, and something very important must have brought this man there.

Then a fear went through his mind. Could it be the prefect of police come to arrest him? And he wished he had not run away that morning to watch the skaters on the ice-bound Vistula.

The man had stepped out of the carriage and was coming up the steps now, looking straight at Frédéric with his dark, piercing eyes. Yes, surely it must be the police official, and the boy wanted to run away and hide. But before he had a chance even to turn, the stranger called to him.

"Are you Frédéric Chopin?" he asked.

And Frédéric was so badly frightened he could hardly answer.

"Yes; but please, please don't take me this time!" he begged, as his eyes filled with tears. "I'll never run away again."

At his words and actions the man looked

much surprised, and spoke as if to explain something:

"Why, I did n't—"

But before he had time to finish the sentence Madame Chopin opened the door. Seeing her little lad in tears, she did not know what it meant.

But Niemcewicz told her what Frédéric had said. Then she knew all about it—knew how badly frightened he was at the thought of going to prison, and she laid her hand lovingly on his dark curls.

Niemcewicz stood looking at her gentle eyes—they were dark, and big and brilliant like Frédéric's—and he thought what a fair woman she was.

"Poor little Frédéric!" she said in a voice that was like low music. "He ran away this morning to watch the skaters on the river, which is a very dangerous pastime for little boys, because horses might tread them underfoot or the city streets swallow them up and lose them; and his father declared that if it ever happened again he would surely put it into the hands of the police. But I think it never will."

And Frédéric's big eyes looked bigger and darker than ever.

"No, it never will," he promised; "so please let me go this time. I did n't mean to be bad, truly I did n't. I could n't help going, because I knew they would sing as they skated, and I love to hear their songs."

And Madame Chopin nodded her head, because she knew it was true. Niemcewicz nodded too, for he, like all Warsaw, had heard that Frédéric loved music as butterflies love sunshine, and his voice was almost as gentle as the mother's when he spoke.

"Don't be afraid," he comforted. "I did n't come to take you to prison, because I am not the prefect of police. And even if I were, I know you'll never run away again. But I did come to see just you, Master Frédéric Chopin."

Which caused Madame Chopin to wonder a very great deal. But she was a gently born woman, and her courtesy was greater than her curiosity. So she invited him to come inside and led the way to the living-room, where the boy's sisters, Emily and Louisa

WONDER-CHILD OF WARSAW 179

and Justinia, were bending over their embroidery.

It was a small room and plainly furnished, not at all like the ones to which the poet was accustomed; but brightness and cheer were there, and he knew it was not just an abiding place but a home. The cat nodded beside the piano-stool that was Frédéric's wonted place, and over the instrument hung a fine old painting, brought by Nicholas Chopin from France when he came to Warsaw some fifteen years before. For he was a son of the Southland, of the sweet, green country of Lorraine, who had married a Polish woman. So in Frédéric's veins were mingled the warm, red blood of the Latin and the warm, red blood of the Slav, both of whom see visions and dream dreams.

The fire on the open hearth sent long bright tongues up toward the chimney, and as they walked near it, Niemcewicz spoke some words to Madame Chopin that the children did not understand. But certainly they were pleasant words; for when they were finished, the mother threw her arms about the boy and exclaimed, "Frédéric, this is Pan [Mr.] Niemcewicz, come to ask you to play at a concert."

And he was as much surprised as he had been frightened a few moments before. No prison cell for him, but a lovely invitation!

"Yes," the man spoke; "and if you do, you will be helping the poor of Warsaw, because all the ticket money is to be given to them."

And the big dark eyes brightened as he said: "Oh, I should like that! Please let me do it, Mother. Please!"

And the smile on Madame Chopin's face said, as plainly as words could say, "Yes."

So it was decided, and a little later the poet Niemcewicz went out of the house and drove away through the whirling snow, leaving behind him Emily and Louisa and Justinia much excited. It would be very splendid to have their brother play before the great of Warsaw, and they wanted to go out and spread the news throughout the neighborhood.

But Frédéric wasn't excited at all. Of course it was delightful to think of helping the poor, but he had played before people so often that it seemed just a usual event. And not until the next day, when his father brought home a new suit for him to wear, did it seem like a great occasion. But at sight of the velvet coat and broad white collar with its frill of lace he wanted the concert to begin immediately so he could wear them, and thought Pan Niemcewicz must be a sort of fairy godfather, for, if he had n't come to ask him to play, the splendid clothes would not have been bought. It was still fifteen days until the appointed night, and it seemed as if they would never pass. He began to think that men who say February is the shortest month in the year are mistaken, and that surely it is the longest, for although the day would wane and the night would come, there was always another day and then another night, and still no concert time. But at last the much desired occasion came, and arrayed in his velvet suit with its splendid collar he walked across the stage of the concert-hall, as proud as a young prince.

The great lords and ladies in the audience looked surprised. He was small for his age, and so slender and delicate that he looked younger than he was, and one powerful noble said in a loud whisper, "Why does Niemcewicz bring us to hear a baby when he might have had a man who could play well?"

And he expected to be very much annoyed.

Little Frédéric sat down and began to play, first somewhat hesitatingly, for the piano was not the accustomed one of his home, and the action was a trifle strange. But in a moment the keys and his fingers seemed to understand each other, and he played as never a child of Warsaw had played before. The lords and ladies in the audience sat very straight and very still, and, when he finished, applauded with hand and voice. Even the Grand Duke Constantine, who seldom gave praise to any one, called "Bravo! bravo!" while the noble who had blamed Niemcewicz for bringing the boy there, sought the poet's side and exclaimed, "Surely he is Poland's wonder-child, even as little Mozart was Austria's! Have him come out again!"

So the child played again to the silently listening throng, after which the applause thundered once more and some of the ladies had tears in their eyes.

WONDER-CHILD OF WARSAW 183

And what thought little Frédéric? Oh, he was very much pleased. He was too young to understand how marvelous was the music that he had made, and thought they applauded because they liked his clothes. So a little later, when he went home and his mother asked him which number the people liked best, he said, "Oh, Mama, everybody was looking at my collar."

But he was much mistaken, for most of them had n't noticed his collar. They saw only a wonder-child with a mop of curly hair and eyes like living jewels.

A year passed, and many times since that concert had carriages of noblemen come to the humble Chopin house. The high-born folk of Warsaw petted the little musician and made his life very bright, and he had so many invitations that his mother said he no longer belonged to her, but to all of Poland; which was true, for a genius belongs not only to his family, but to his country and the world. His father was only a teacher and not rich, but very often the boy went as a guest to some splendid castle of his land, where he lived the life of a young noble, and Polish nobles of those days lived luxuriously indeed. They loved his sunny youth and joyous ways; loved the melody he drew from the piano; and always, when they heard him, said that some day he would bring honor to his name and glory to Poland.

Then something happened that brought him both joy and sorrow.

It was January, and Catalani, a great Italian singer, with a voice of gold and a face of ivory and rose, came into snow-wrapped Warsaw. Great was the excitement there, for Poland was a music-loving land, and she was the empress of song of her day. Up from Italy she came to sing the melodies of the South in the frozen North; and people talked of it in the streets and at the public meeting-places.

"We will fill the concert-hall," said one, "and prove to her that we Poles love the best."

"Yes," his neighbor answered, "and we will take our children to hear her too, so that long after childhood is past they will remember Catalini, the great singer."

One of the first to hear the news was Nicholas Chopin.

"It is rare good fortune for us of Warsaw," he announced as they sat at supper that night. "She will give four concerts here in the town hall."

At the words Frédéric gave a shout.

"Catalani to sing!" he exclaimed. "Oh, Father, I want to hear her!"

And the big man nodded in reply.

"That you shall, my Frédéric, because I know it will make you very happy."

And Frédéric's heart beat faster at the thought that he was to hear the greatest singer of her time, and one of the greatest of all time. Nothing so wonderful had happened in his short life, not even when he played at the charity concert and wore his velvet suit and lace-trimmed collar. And as he sat beside his mother, among the great lords and ladies assembled in the music-hall on the eventful night, he scarcely breathed, for Catalani was singing, and all the jewels, all the flowers, and all the gorgeous colors ever dreamed of seemed mingled in her tones, and, as they floated out, wonderful pictures passed before his eyes. Sometimes it seemed as if a thousand streams purled over a rainbow meadow, sometimes as if elves and sprites were floating through the air. He shut his eyes, but still he saw the pictures, which seemed very strange. For he did not know that the rainbow colors were not in the concert-hall, but in his own soul, and were painted there by the music because he was a wonder-child.

Thrice after that night he heard Catalani sing, and every time he dreamed dreams and went off into that realm whose gates open only to those who have rainbows in their souls. Then, like the most beautiful dream of all, she asked him to play for her. Niemcewicz the poet brought the news, and although he seemed a sort of fairy godfather who could make anything come to pass, Frédéric could hardly believe it was true. For how could the golden-voiced singer know of a lad like him? But she did know, because the Grand Duke Constantine and other great folk of Warsaw had told her all about him, and she wanted to hear the music of the

WONDER-CHILD OF WARSAW 187

boy who was called a wonder-child. So he was dressed in his best, just as he was dressed the night of the charity concert, and drove away to the castle in whose music-room he was to play.

A throng of noble folk welcomed him, and the great piano there responded like a living thing to the magic of his fingers. Catalani heard, and, hearing, thought with the others that he was, indeed, a wonder-child; and when he finished, she applauded and said as lovely things as song-loving Warsaw said about her singing, which made him very happy. Then regal Princess Lowica, the Grand Duke Constantine, Count and Countess Skarbeck, and golden-haired Countess Potocka came close to the piano, saying gracious things and petting him so that he seemed like a little king receiving homage, and all in all it was the most splendid holiday he had ever known.

But suddenly the blue went out of his skies and the music out of his world, for Catalani asked him to tell her his birthday. That seemed a terrible thing, for although he could do wonders at the piano, he could n't remember his birthday, no matter how hard he tried. His mother had told him over and over again, but he always got it mixed, and did n't know if it was the twelfth of February or the twenty-second, or the twenty-second of March.

So he hung his head and said, "I don't know, but one is coming soon."

At which all the lords and ladies laughed, and the singer remarked, "I must surely find out when it is!"

He was so full of shame about it that he had to bite his lips to keep back the tears, and, as he drove home with Niemcewicz, though the sun was shining and the skies clear, everything looked black and cloudy to him. Catalani, golden-voiced Catalani, would think him a stupid, and he had been so eager to have her like him. But there were some things little Frédéric did n't know.

Madame Catalani had said she would find out when his birthday came, and find out she did, for early in the morning of that day a messenger came to the house where more than a year before Niemcewicz the poet had

He scarcely breathed, for Catalani was singing

WONDER-CHILD OF WARSAW 191

come to ask a big-eyed boy to play at a charity concert. He struck the iron knocker on the door, spoke a few words to Emily, and went away; and a minute later Madame Chopin called, "A package for you, Frédéric."

Frédéric came on the run, as any boy would do when it is his birthday and packages come. Then he pulled off the wrapper and saw something that made his eyes dance.

"A watch, Mother, a watch!" he shouted.

And upon the shining gold case was engraved the date and the words, "Given by Madame Catalani to Frédéric Chopin, aged ten years."

Which made him so glad that he broke into a dance that his sister Louisa said was neither polonaise nor mazurka, but the mother knew it was a dance of joy. "Oh!" he exclaimed, "oh, oh, oh! She likes me even if I did n't know."

And he stood by the window looking out across the snow, seeing in memory the singer of the Southland with her face of ivory and rose.

Well, from that day forth Frédéric remembered his birthday. Who would n't with a watch like that? For whenever he forgot, one look set him right, and he went on thinking Catalani was one of the sweetest women in the world as well as the most glorious singer. And he worked at his music, too, playing more wonderfully than any child had played since the boy Mozart, until, when he grew older and went to seek his fortune in Paris, the great of the French capital honored the man as the great of Warsaw had honored the boy; and there was no home so splendid or so exclusive that it shut its doors to him.

But he was always the slender, delicate man, just as he was the slender, delicate child whose frail appearance almost made the poet Niemcewiez think he was not the lad he sought; and he died at the early age of forty. But sometimes, when the heart is great and full, short lives are as rich in achievement as those that stretch out to four score years and ten. And so it was with Chopin. He gave more to the world than many have given who have lived to be twice his age, because nothing but his best seemed fine enough to give, and of that he wanted to give abundantly.

WONDER-CHILD OF WARSAW 193

So with infinite care and patience he labored to make each composition nobler and more beautiful than the preceding one, more nearly what seemed to be the perfect fruit of his soul and brain.

And he never ceased to love his Slavic land. Memories of his childhood home in Warsaw, of the quaint old houses and winding streets, of the nobles in whose castles he had spent so many golden hours, of the shimmering, restless Vistula, where peasants sang as they rocked in their boats through summer twilights, sang too as they whirled on the glistening ice in the long white winters, were ever with the exile there in Paris, and were ever dear—so dear that he made his best music when his heart was in Poland.

More than sixty years have passed since his melody-making ended and he went to his rest beside Bellini and Cherubini in quiet Père Lachaise. But his music still lives on, still is loved, is exquisitely beautiful. For beauty, like truth and goodness, is immortal; and as long as the world loves melody, it will revere the name of that wonder-child of Warsaw, Frédéric Chopin.

THE LIGHT OF GUIDO'S LAMP

XI

THE LIGHT OF GUIDO'S LAMP

THE street was as silent as a deserted place, for it was midnight, and the only human sound that broke the velvet stillness was the slow, measured tread of Cambisti the town crier, as he tramped up and down on his beat. Now he cast eye along the via at the homes of the populace, now across toward the Gothic towers of the Bolognini Palace, that rose ghostly gray among the chestnut trees, crying "All 's well! All 's well!" And all *was* well, for the ducal guards were alert in every danger place, and the people of Bologna slept.

Suddenly he stopped and stared with wondering eyes. Out from a window above him shone a streak of light, not strong and brilliant, like the gleam of the many tapers Bologna folk used to brighten their festive halls, but a weak, pale ray, as if from a single fat lamp. It came from the home of Reni the musician, and the crier thought it strange, for he knew Master Daniele had gone early to his house that evening, saying he was tired and wanted to get to rest.

"Mayhap some one is ill and needs ministering unto," he thought. And that he might not disturb a suffering one, he went quietly down the street without calling out in his accustomed way.

The next morning he met Master Reni in the Piazza del Nettuno, and asked him the meaning of the lamp in the night. The musician seemed much surprised.

"What do you mean?" he questioned. "No one was ill in my house and no lamp burned there."

But when Cambisti insisted he had seen a gleam from the window, Daniele looked frightened.

"Can it be that thieves were in," he exclaimed, and asked the crier to go with him and find out.

But there was no trace of pilfering in the house. Nothing was missing nor had been

THE LIGHT OF GUIDO'S LAMP 199

disturbed, and then the musician laughed heartily at the watchman.

"A fine employee of the duke you are," he teased. "You sleep on your beat and see things in dreams. It must be so, for now I am convinced that no light burned in my house last night."

Although Cambisti did not understand it, he did not press the subject. He had no liking for being the butt of any man's jokes, and he knew the ray from Master Reni's window was no dream light. He made up his mind to watch again, for the musician's conduct had aroused his suspicions, and he wondered if his fear of thieves had been feigned. It might be that some dark plot was being concocted there, for certain men of the populace had lately berated the ruling of the Duke of Bologna, and although Master Daniele was not suspected of being of the number, he would watch and find out, as befitted a town crier. So as soon as darkness fell, he betook him to the street by the musician's house.

Three times, five, seven, he walked to the spot and peered up at the window from which the light had shone the night before, but not the faintest ray pierced the darkness. He decided that pilferers had gone there, and finding nothing to their liking, departed without leaving any trace—or, as Master Reni had said, maybe he *had* slept on his beat and dreamed of the light. And thus musing, he started down the street.

Just then the hour bell in the castle tower rang, and turning in the direction of the sound he happened to look toward the Reni windows. His eyes opened wide, and he stood and stared, for shining out, just as it had shone the night before, was a pale, faint light. "So," he murmured. "Cambisti does not dream on his beat, after all, as Master Reni shall learn."

And hurrying up to the door, he rattled the knocker.

The musician was sleeping soundly when the thumping on the sash awakened him, and as he detested being roused from sleep, he went scowling and grumbling to the door.

"What idiot comes at this hour to disturb an honest man's rest?" he muttered as he thrust back the bolt.

THE LIGHT OF GUIDO'S LAMP 201

"Master Daniele," Cambisti said in a whisper, "just step outside and find out whether I dream of lights or see them."

Reni was thoroughly awake now, and a little alarmed. Still, he half believed the man had turned demented.

"It would be small wonder if he had," he thought as he followed him down the steps, "with twenty years of town crying."

But suddenly that idea went out of his head. No, the night watch was in full possession of his senses. A light shone from the window just as he had said. Thieves must be abroad, and he shivered, for the ray came from his little son's room.

"And he but a baby, too," he thought.

They held a whispered consultation about what to do, decided to summon help, and go to the place where the light burned. So Reni ran to the house of a neighbor and Cambisti to call some soldiers of the guard. It would be folly for an unarmed citizen and a town crier who was no longer young to go into the house alone, for well they knew the terrible nature of the dreaded Bologna banditti, who were skilled in the use of sword and halberd and whose blows were swift and sure. Such men did not venture into possible danger without being prepared for it, and they who surprised them in their evil doing must be strong and ready, for it meant a battle.

Five minutes later six soldiers, the night watch, and the two citizens crept up the narrow stairway that led from the street. They were not cowards, these men of Bologna, yet they trembled a bit at the thought of the possible fate that awaited them in the lighted room. Cautiously, silently moving, they reached the door, and each poised his weapon ready to strike as Cambisti thrust it open.

Then, what a sight met their eyes! In the middle of the floor, smiling as if the joy of the world were in his heart, a curly-haired child bent over a paper, drawing by the light of a fat lamp. It was Reni's nine-year-old son, and he was so absorbed in what he was doing that he did not see the group standing behind him, or turn from his work until his father exclaimed, "Guido!"

Then he glanced up, and noticing the

THE LIGHT OF GUIDO'S LAMP 203

armed men, looked in a startled way from one to the other. But before he could ask what it meant, Daniele Reni questioned sharply, "What are you doing there?"

A look of terror flashed across his face, for his father's angry voice and the presence of the soldiers were something he could not understand. He caught up the paper over which he had been bending as if it were a precious thing, and his lip quivered as he answered, "Making pictures."

Daniele Reni was more severe than ever.

"Where did you get that lamp?" he demanded.

Guido did not drop his eyes as if he felt guilty and had something to conceal, but looked steadily into his father's face, replying, "I bought it with my birthday money. Uncle Vittorio told me to spend it for the thing I liked best."

The musician walked close, looking sternly at his son.

"A fine way for you to make a laughing stock of me!" he thundered. "Now get you back to bed."

And blowing out the light, he took the

lamp with him, and he and his companions went down-stairs, while the child behind in the dark wondered what it all meant.

As soon as they were beyond Guido's hearing Cambisti and the soldiers laughed uproariously, but Reni did not share their merriment. He scowled and frowned as they talked, picturing to himself how the townsfolk would jeer him when the word was noised abroad.

"It's no mirthful thing to me!" he exclaimed. "That lad cares for nothing but drawing. I wish him to be a musician, which is the calling of the men of my house, but he seems worthless and will not stay at the harpsichord. Thinking to break him of his everlasting picture-making I took paper away from him, but he marked on the walls at night. Then his mother hid the lamp and made him go to bed in the dark, but he has contrived to get another and some more drawing stuff, and what I am to do with him baffles me."

The soldiers nodded sympathetically, and Cambisti and the neighbor went away, thankful that God had sent them daughters instead

THE LIGHT OF GUIDO'S LAMP 205

of boys who might worry them as young Guido worried Daniele.

At that time Bologna was the seat of one of the most elegant and cultured courts of Italy. Nowhere were there finer concerts than in the great hall of the Bolognini Palace, nowhere were there nobler paintings, more exquisite statues, or more splendid tapestries than those possessed by the ducal family. The lord of the province was a lover of art, and creators in every line were invited to his capitol. Thus it happened that Daniele Reni, whose musical ability was recognized throughout Bologna, was summoned to the royal seat one day to assist with his bagpipes at a concert. It was less than a week after they found Guido drawing in the night, and his wife suggested that he take the lad with him.

"Perhaps the fine music he hears will lead him to care for the harpsichord," she remarked as she made the proposition.

Daniele nodded agreement, thinking it a good idea, and a few hours later when he went to the royal residence young Guido trotted along beside him.

The boy was very happy in the thought of going to the palace, and his father was pleased, for he believed the idea of hearing the splendid music delighted him. But although Master Reni was a good piper he was a poor guesser, and did not know what was in his son's mind. If he had, he would have left him at home.

To the lad the trip meant a sight of glorious pictures, a glimpse of the works of the master painters of Italy. He knew the Duke of Bologna loved music, but he knew he loved color too, and that was why his eyes gleamed so pleasurably as he and his father hurried along the via.

They did not stop to look at any of the sights along the way, although it was Maytime and the gardens were gay in their blossom dresses. Rapidly they walked along the broad Via Castiglione, past the rich gateways and imposing colonnades of the Pepoli Palace, until the spacious piazza of Santo Stefano spread out before them. Beyond, majestic in its Gothic splendor, was the Bolognini Palace, set in the midst of a park whose beauty was celebrated from the Alps

THE LIGHT OF GUIDO'S LAMP

to the Bay of Naples. Daniele Reni told his son he might play under the trees until a page summoned him into the concert hall, for a rehearsal was to precede the performance, and he wanted the boy to hear the music in its perfection rather than in the crudity of the making.

Young Guido liked the idea much, for there was many a fountain and grotto and bit of copsewood there that he wanted to examine. In his delight at finding so many interesting things he forgot that he had been told to stay close to the Santo Stefano entrance, and began to ramble about as if he had the entire day to spend in the garden. Now it was a sculptured fountain that claimed his attention, now a trellised path along which ladies of the castle went on their way to the bath, now an aviary where tropical birds flashed their gorgeous plumage, vying in color and splendor with the roses and pomegranate flowers beyond.

Now it happened that the Lord of Bologna not only patronized artists by inviting them to give concerts at the palace and embellishing his halls with their work, but sometimes he gave them apartments and board and keep, that they might be free to create unworried by the thought of rent and food bills. Not long before Dionisio Calvart, a famous Flemish painter, had established a workshop and school under the protection of the beauty-loving noble, and young Guido, in the course of his ramble, came upon his studio.

The lad felt that he had entered a wonderland. His eyes flashed as he saw the marvels of brush and color there, his face brightened as if electrified, and one of Dionisio's pupils, seeing the delight which his every look and gesture expressed, called the teacher.

Calvart turned from his canvas and looked at the boy, who was standing before a madonna, making strokes with his hands as if they held an imaginary brush, studying every line and hue of the pictured face.

"What are you doing?" the painter asked kindly, wondering at such interest being shown by one so young.

THE LIGHT OF GUIDO'S LAMP 209

Guido turned toward him with wonder-wide eyes.

"Oh, the picture!" he exclaimed. "If only I could paint like that! If only father would let me try!"

Master Calvart left his work and went over to where the lad stood.

"Do you want to be a painter?" he asked.

Guido nodded.

"Indeed I do. But father is a musician, and says I must be one too. He took my things away so I could n't draw any pictures but those I made in the dust. Then Uncle Vittorio gave me some birthday money, and I bought a lamp and paper and worked at night. But he took that, too, before I had a chance to finish my drawings."

And he pulled from his blouse a roll of papers and held them up for the artist to see.

Calvart examined them curiously, and asked how old he was.

"Nine last week," Guido replied. "My birthday is just past."

Again the man looked at the drawings, murmuring, "Only nine! The wonder of it!"

His approval was so evident to the pupils that they turned from their work and gazed from boy to master, eager to know what he would say next.

There was a sound of footsteps in the corridor outside, and a moment later the duke came into the studio. All rose to greet him, and Calvart put the drawings into his hand.

"See what this boy has done," he said. "He tells me he is just nine."

Little Guido was much surprised. Were they very good or very bad, he wondered, that the painter showed them to the duke.

The Lord of Bologna understood art as well as he loved it. For a moment he studied the drawings, then spoke in a kindly voice.

"You did them without help?" he asked.

"Yes, sire," Guido replied.

Then, as other questions were put, he told the story of his struggle to draw.

"So you are the son of Daniele Reni?" the noble remarked. "Well, we will see about it."

THE LIGHT OF GUIDO'S LAMP

Suddenly Guido happened to remember he was to have waited in the park near the Santo Stefano gate.

"Oh!" he exclaimed in dismay. "Father will be angry with me. Maybe he has sent for me already."

The Duke of Bologna laid his hand on the boy's shoulder.

"Have no fear," he spoke. "I'll take you to your father, and I promise you he will not be angry with you."

So together they went, and imagine the surprise of Daniele Reni, just as the pipers were beginning the opening number, to see his boy Guido enter the music hall with the Lord of Bologna. And both man and child smiled happily, so it could not be that he had gotten into mischief about the castle. What did it mean?

He did not have to wonder long, for the duke stopped the concert to ask him a question.

"Is this your son, Reni?" he inquired.

"Yes," the amazed man answered.

The noble turned to the boy.

"Now tell him, and tell him the truth," he

said. "Do you want to be an artist or a musician?"

Young Guido's eyes darkened with earnestness as he spoke.

"Sire, I want to be a painter," came the reply.

Then, turning to the father, the duke asked, "What think you of it, Daniele?"

The man at the bagpipe shook his head.

"It is my wish that he be a musician and follow the calling of the men of my house, which to my notion is a most noble one."

The great noble mused for a moment, while the people wondered what would happen next. He was a kindly man, and wanted to persuade, even though he had the authority to command. So he said gently, "To be sure, yours is a noble calling, but that of the painter is noble also, and since your boy shows such aptitude for being a son of brush and canvas, why not let him follow his desire and become one?"

It was a difficult moment for the father, for ever since Guido was born he had dreamed he would be a musician, a better and more successful one than he had been, and

THE LIGHT OF GUIDO'S LAMP 213

hopes of years are not put aside easily. But he was a sensible man, and a kindly one, and although his eyes were sad his face held a smile as he answered, "So be it, for I have no wish to warp my boy's career. A painter he shall become, if only he will be a good one."

"That only the years can prove," the duke replied, "but it is my belief that they will tell a wonderful story."

Thus, young Guido Reni came to be apprenticed to the artist Calvart. Thus, as an old-time biographer says, "He passed from the concert of voice to the concert of colors."

Rich, eventful days followed that morning when he roamed from the Bolognini garden into the studio of the palace, for his passion for work and the rapidity of his progress was amazing to teacher and fellow pupils. Soon he began to draw from reliefs and from life, and four years later, when only thirteen, had advanced so far that Calvart appointed him to teach, and it seemed that the prophecy of the Lord of Bologna would be fulfilled.

By the time he was eighteen he painted

backgrounds for all the pictures in the studio, and often his work, after being slightly retouched, was sold as the master's own. His fellow pupils thought he had learned all it was possible for an art student to learn, but Guido had no such idea. He knew there are no play places on the road to success, and constantly he toiled and studied. He visited other studios, especially that of the Caracci Brothers, then among the most illustrious painters of Italy, observing all that was best in their work and striving to put it into his own. After a time Calvart became jealous of the pupil who already excelled him, criticized his pictures unkindly, and one day rubbed out his most careful work. Guido knew it was far better than much that had won the master's praise, and could not bear such injustice. So he fled from the studio and became a pupil of the Caracci.

From that time forth his progress was almost phenomenal. He began filling orders, and his work was so pleasing to his patrons that they wanted him to paint other pictures and still others, until it seemed he would eclipse the Caracci even as he had eclipsed

THE LIGHT OF GUIDO'S LAMP

Calvart. In fact, one day when Ludovicio was instructing him how to paint the flesh of little children, Annibale, one of the brothers, cried, "Do not teach that fellow so much, or some day he will know more than the whole of us! He is never contented, but continually searches into new matters. Remember, Ludovicio, some day this fellow will make you sigh."

And the prophecy came true. In a very short time young Guido Reni was the glory of Bologna, and then he went to Rome, where he worked as steadily and painstakingly as he had worked in the studio of Calvart. One idea he kept ever before him—the perfect picture—and no matter how splendid a work seemed, or how much praise it received from patrons and critics, he would not let it leave his hand as long as he saw the tiniest detail that could be improved.

Believing his chosen calling to be the noblest in the world, he tried to make every effort worthy of it. He was proud of being of the brotherhood of painters, and had no patience with those of his colleagues who fawned at the feet of royalty, grateful for any favor the high born chose to bestow. One day he was walking with the sculptor Cordiere, who suddenly stepped into the street and ambled along beside the coach of Cardinal Borghese, to tell him of some work he was doing. Guido refused to join him, and when his friend returned to his side, berated him soundly for having acted like a menial.

"How can you expect to win the esteem of the Pope and the highest in the land," he said, "since you trot so contentedly after a cardinal's carriage? Such conduct is not seemly for men of our profession."

Hundreds of commissions came to him in Rome, among them being one to fresco the casino of the Rospigliosi Palace. Guido went to work with all his wonted zeal, determined to create something finer than he had done before, and he succeeded so triumphantly that when the task was finished all of Rome marveled at his achievement, just as the world has marveled at it ever since. For he had painted "The Aurora," that glorious masterpiece in which the god of day,

THE LIGHT OF GUIDO'S LAMP 217

attended by a group of dancing Hours, dashes along in his chariot beside a turquoise sea to usher in the morning. Yes, the years were telling their story, just as the Lord of Bologna believed they would.

This great fresco established Guido as the idol of Italy and the master painter of his day. Commissions came to him in such numbers that he could not execute half of them, while many other artists were idle. And so it was throughout his long, eventful career. One brilliant success followed another. One noble creation paved the way for something nobler, and like one inspired he toiled and achieved. Often he had to contend with the jealousies of less gifted painters, but usually the kindliness of his nature overcame them. He was courted like a lord of the land—in fact, the mightiest of Italy paid him homage, and once, as he returned to Rome from a visit to Bologna, the carriages of princes and cardinals met him at the Ponte Molle, on the Flaminian Way, each vying with the other for the honor of bearing him into the capital. The high born of the Imperial City pointed with pride to his house, saying, "Yonder lives Master Reni, the painter."

When he died his body was borne to its resting place amid pomp and ceremony seldom seen even in Rome, the pompous city. Knights and prelates in splendid attire, laborers and artisans, men, women, and children of all ranks and ages, thronged the street through which the procession moved on its way to the church of San Domenico— "So many," one of the old chroniclers states, "that the like of it was never seen before, not even when Rome celebrated its deliverance from the plague." Every one mourned the passing of the artist and man, for he had been kindly, charitable, and magnanimous, and numbered friends among all classes. Thousands that day thought of the kind deeds done and favors granted by him, who, though lionized by all of Italy, never lost his graciousness and human sympathy. And men think of them still as they marvel at the beauty of his works.

Thus, the years told a wonderful story. Thus, through the glory of his pictures, the light of Guido's lamp shines down the ages,

THE LIGHT OF GUIDO'S LAMP

and helps to brighten the world to-day, just as three centuries ago the ray beheld by the night watchman gleamed through the darkness of old Bologna town.

OLD JAN'S TWILIGHT TALE

XII

OLD JAN'S TWILIGHT TALE

HIS face was wrinkled and his back was bent and his step was faltering and slow, but he was the best story-teller in all Copenhagen, and wherever he went a group of children followed until he seemed like another Pied Piper. In all his seventy years he had not grown too old to have an interest in their sports and games, nor was he ever too busy to refuse a bit of advice when they asked it. That is why he put aside the book he was reading and went out on the stoop, for just then merry voices sounded in from the street and he knew the neighborhood boys and girls were having a frolic there.

They saw him as he came out of the doorway, and one of the number called blithely, "Ah, there's Jan now! I wonder if he has a story for us?"

And with a rush and bound they surrounded him and began a chorus of pleas.

"A sea story," called gray-eyed Charlotte Ruleson, whose father was a boatman, and who had heard many of the weird yarns floating about among sailor folk; "one with pirates and lots of shooting." While another begged for a ghost tale with a big spook, and still another wanted a fairy story with witches and goblins and all those creatures who play pranks in Elfland. Each had his request for the kind of tale he liked best, but one slender boy, with a shock of yellow hair and a face like a youthful viking, said nothing. He just stood and watched the old man, with a look of pleading in his lobelia-blue eyes.

Jan saw it, and knew that he, too, had his desire, but for some reason had not voiced it. So he turned to him and asked, "And you, Bertel Thorwaldsen, what do you want?"

As he spoke, a smile of rare sweetness came over the lad's strong face, and he answered in a voice that was low and vibrant, "A hunting story, if you please; one of the days when you were in India."

A chorus of laughter sounded from the

group, and smiles and grimaces were on almost every face.

"You might know he'd ask for something about animals," exclaimed Christine Jacobsen. "Most of the time he isn't sketching he puts in watching them, and the other day the school-master said if he knew half as much about his lessons as he knows about horses and cattle, he wouldn't get the ferule so often. You'd think he'd get over dreaming about them when they get him into trouble."

"Yes, especially after what they did for him to-day," remarked Hals Sorensen. "He forgot to take his father's dinner because he was at the Amalienborg making a picture of the king's riding horse, and poor Gottshalk Thorwaldsen had to go without eating after working all morning over his figure-heads. So now there's talk of taking Master Bertel out of school and sending him to Jutland to work in the fields."

"We all know that, Hals Sorensen," Christine broke in, "so I don't see why you need tell it again. My mother says it's a pity, too, because Bertel has a real talent for drawing, and if his father 'd only let him help with his figure-heads his own work would be better and people would stop saying he has a no-account son."

Christine's mother was the daughter of an artist, so the girl knew that when a love of drawing is born with one he can no more put it aside than he can do without air and water. Her sympathy and understanding had often smoothed the boy's path when his comrades ridiculed him, and he looked at her now with kindly eyes.

Jan, too, smiled at her, because loyalty is always admirable, and he liked her defense of the boy. He knew all about the forgotten dinner and the gossip among the men in the shipyard, that Bertel ought to be taken from school and put to farming, for he worked there himself and had urged the father not to be too hard on the lad while all the others recommended punishment. With all his wrinkles and white hair he still had enough youth in his heart to know that the best-meaning boys sometimes forget, and had sufficient faith to believe that Bertel's knowing his father had gone hungry was a punish-

"And you, Bertel Thorwaldsen, what do you want?"

OLD JAN'S TWILIGHT TALE 229

ment that would keep him from forgetting in the future. Always before he had come in good time with the pail, and often, while the elder Thorwaldsen ate, would correct the drawings from which were carved figureheads for merchant vessels, and many a piece of work was better because of the boy's touch. A lad like that, he reasoned, was not bad at heart, and it was well to be lenient with him for once. So he spoke very kindly.

"I know all about it, Hals," he said, "but I believe Bertel has had his lesson, and it won't happen again. I am sure his father thinks so too, because just before I came home to-night he told me that after this he intends to take him to the shipyard every day to help with the cuts, which will be far better than working in the Jutland fields. So let us talk of something that will make no one unhappy."

And quieting their remarks, they sat down beside him to listen to a story.

Away to the north the sky glowed with a soft pink light, as if a sheet of rose leaves had been spread across it, and downward, from the mass of color, streamers like variegated ribbons floated toward the horizon, faint at first, but fast deepening to the gray that comes with the approach of night, and Jan watched the changing tints with dreamy eyes. Bertel's request for a hunting story had brought memories of twilight tints in other skies, and of the far-off time when every day was filled with thrilling adventure. For he had not always been a cargo loader in the Copenhagen shipyard, but once had traveled in distant lands and hunted game with the best sports of Europe. But he was old now, and the most exciting things life held were the evening visits of the children, to whom the tales of the one-time wanderer were like the pages of some splendid romance. So he began a story of his Indian days, one which he said was the most vividly remembered of all his hunting experiences.

Blue-eyed Bertel moved closer, and sat with glowing eyes as the old man described, in a picturesque way, the jungle where he had hunted in his youth. The boy could almost see the trees with their trailing moss, the lush, tropical vines that swung ropes of bloom from the branches, and the banyan

OLD JAN'S TWILIGHT TALE 231

thicket, made hideous at night by the cries of savage beasts. He had often heard of how the natives hunted with javelins, and how, when the first European sportsmen came, they acted as guides to the strangers, but it was all new and thrilling when recounted by the one-time huntsman.

Jan then told of a guide sighting a lion, a magnificent creature that well might have been the king of all that jungle.

"The fellow sent his javelin at him, and struck the beast full in the breast. And, ever since that day, I think of a lion, not as a wild creature of the woods, but as one guarding with his life all it holds most dear. Because," he went on, "his mate was just beyond with her two cubs, and as the iron struck him he lunged forward, with defiance in his eyes, as if to say, 'You shall not harm them until you have killed me.'"

Bertel thought a great deal about the story, and for a long time afterward, when men talked of bravery, he saw a lion in the Indian jungle, standing with a javelin in its breast, yet defying the hunters to touch its mate and little ones. And often when he went to visit

Jan he would ask him to repeat the tale. Then, some one, seeing him at work on the figure-heads in the shipyard, persuaded his father that such talent for drawing and carving ought to be cultivated and he was sent to the Royal Academy of Fine Arts. Throughout that winter there were sketches to be made in the evenings, so there was no time for visits. Before summer came Jan died, and there were no more twilight tales. But he remembered those he had heard, and, most vividly of all, that of the wounded lion in the Indian jungle.

Years passed, with summers of Denmark's lovely twilights and winters made glorious by northern lights. Bertel still worked at his drawing, and at carving too, modeling figures he hoped some day to fashion in marble. But marble costs much money, and Thorwaldsen was poor. He went to Rome, hoping in that home of art to find some one who would give him an order, that he might prove what he could do. But no order came. Still he worked on undaunted, even when the first model of his "Jason" crumbled into fragments because he was too poor to have

OLD JAN'S TWILIGHT TALE 233

it cast. He struggled on until it seemed useless to hope longer. Then, heart broken and discouraged, he packed his trunk to return to Copenhagen.

But it was not meant for Bertel Thorwaldsen to die unknown. An English banker, whose name, by the way, was Hope, heard of the artist, and came to see his work. To Thorwaldsen he seemed as good as his name, for he gave him an order for a statue, which was so finely executed that the genius discovered long before in the Copenhagen shipyard came to be recognized all over Europe. Order after order came, and he carved so rapidly and exquisitely that the whole world was amazed. Not since the days of the old masters had any wrought such wonders with chisels and marble, and he was called to almost every continental city that wished to erect a splendid statue. The Danes, who had thought him a worthless fellow, no longer talked about Gottshalk's no-account son, but spoke proudly of "Our Thorwaldsen."

Just as he was rising to his zenith, Switzerland was eager to erect a monument to the memory of her children who had died in defense of the Tuileries. All the world knows how, when Louis XVI was taken before the assembly that was to deprive him of his power, a mob attacked the palace. The Swiss guards might have driven it back, but a messenger from the king came with word that they should not fire into the crowd, but were to retire. Within the palace was a handful of warders whom the royal edict did not reach, and they, not knowing of the order, tried to defend the place. But too weak to hold out against the populace, and too faithful to desert their post, they were massacred without mercy. What was more fitting than that the mountain land that nurtured them should raise an undying tribute to their memory?

General Plyffer von Altishofen, an officer of the guard who escaped from the mob, had returned to Lucerne and was living in retirement there. It was his idea to erect a monument to honor his fallen comrades, and he made known his plan.

All Switzerland responded. From every canton, from every lake-gemmed valley, and

OLD JAN'S TWILIGHT TALE 235

upland Alp, came a manifestation of the spirit that has made the country a fitting land of Tell, and the voice of the people said, "We will make it a national monument to our heroic dead."

Funds began to pour in, the amount growing steadily and rapidly until enough was realized to erect something very splendid and very enduring.

"Who shall the sculptor be?" was then the question.

And in answer was asked another question, "Who but Thorwaldsen?"

So to Italy, where the magician of the North was at work, came a call from crystal lake and snow-capped peak that he should come to Lucerne. And to Lucerne he went, to begin the work that was to immortalize him.

But he had a hard problem to solve. What was a theme noble enough to commemorate such heroism? It must be something grandly appropriate, yet different from every monument in the world, for the spirit of patriotism was afire in Switzerland, and nothing commonplace would be considered.

One sketch after another was made, only to be cast aside as being a conception not big and fine enough. Then one night as he lay thinking about it, when the wind whipped the water of the lake until it sounded like the old Baltic beating against his own Danish shores, there came a memory of Jan's twilight tale.

"Standing with a javelin in its breast," the old man had said, "yet defying the hunters to touch its mate and little ones."

Nothing could be more appropriate than that, he thought, and the next day he submitted the design, a wounded lion guarding the escutcheon of France.

The men of the committee were delighted. It was an unusual theme, and worthy of such a memorial. So the model was begun.

Thorwaldsen had never seen a live lion, but that was no insurmountable obstacle to him. He studied old statues for form and proportion, reading, drawing, and working night and day, and when the finished model suited him it was chiseled out of native granite in the general's garden, against a rugged cliff overlooking the lake and facing

OLD JAN'S TWILIGHT TALE 237

the peaks, a fitting tribute to the children of the Alps.

And did Switzerland approve? Ah, yes. The day of its unveiling was made a national holiday. From every canton throngs of people poured into the city, singing the songs of Helvetia and showering honors upon a Northern artist. Yet none knew whence came his inspiration, for not until many years afterward did he reveal the secret. Then, walking one evening with his loved friend, Hans Christian Andersen, he told the cargo-loader's story.

"I was just a lad when I heard it," he said, "but I never forgot it."

Thus it became known that old Jan's tale of a wounded lion in an Indian jungle, told at twilight to a blue-eyed boy in Copenhagen, became the inspiration of the matchless monument that to-day looks out over the clear waters of the Lake of the Four Cantons, and is known the world around as "The Lion of Lucerne."

WHEN THE PRINCESS PASSED

XIII

WHEN THE PRINCESS PASSED

THE little Italian town was gay in its holiday dress, for the Princess was coming. On this smiling morning of early April Veronica Gambara, flower of the house of Pio, was to ride in state to the palace to become the bride of Ghiberto of Correggio, and it seemed that nature vied with man in welcoming her. Under a sky of turquoise, roses red as flame and yellow as the gold of Ophir bloomed in odorous array. A thousand banners swung like pendant rainbows across the line of march, and a thousand gaudy sashes flashed on the waists of village girls. Mummers sang their blithest melodies, and in gardens beyond the crowd larks trilled to the sun. Yes, it was a fitting day for the union of two lordly houses.

Some one gave a shout and the crowd

pressed nearer the street, for the procession was coming, and with eager eyes the people watched the approach of the splendid, stately cavalcade. Now they could see the advance guard of soldiers, now the red uniforms of the outriders, the gilding of the royal coach, and the ivory and purple robes of Veronica, all gorgeous in the sun. Resplendent banners gleamed before and behind her, smiling faces greeted her as she smiled back at them, and cheers rang out the homage of the townsfolk as they nodded to each other saying, "She is well suited to become the Lady of Correggio." But one sturdy peasant lad was gravely silent, although his eyes shone as if they had beheld a vision. He was a stocky, short fellow not quite fourteen, and his name was Antonio Allegri. When the others hurried to the plaza to join in the festivities, he turned toward the cottage of the village baker—a low, stone, whitewashed building with a trellis of climbing roses and a garden plot where grew artichokes and lentils—and people wondered why he went. But they soon forgot about him in thoughts of other things.

All afternoon merriment ran high in the town of Correggio. Up in the palace great folk sat at the wedding feast, and down in the public plaza the townspeople vented their joy in dancing. Those who could afford a present, sent it as a token of good will to Veronica, while those who had nothing to give gathered wayside flowers and piled them before the altar of the Virgin, praying that a blessing might rest on the head of Ghiberto's bride. Every one paid homage to the Princess by joining in the celebration, every one but the baker's boy. He lay in the shadow of the artichokes behind the whitewashed cottage and seemed to be very busy with something.

Toward sundown Catarina, his sister, came from the place of the dancers and went into the house to add a bit of ribbon to her gown. Her cheeks flamed in the joy of the occasion, for it was a day such as Correggio never had seen, and she was glad it came in her time, instead of before or after it. She wondered about Antonio, who had not been to the plaza throughout the afternoon, and failing to find him in the cottage, stood a moment under the roses that crept over the doorway, and then she saw him at the edge of the garden.

"*Fratello mio* (brother mine)," she exclaimed, "why do you not dance with us in honor of the Lady Veronica? It is not right that you fail in homage to the Princess."

The sturdy lad in the peasant smock came toward her as she spoke.

"I do not fail," he replied. "I pay homage to the Princess with a picture."

Catarina clapped her hands.

"A picture!" she exclaimed. "Do let me see it."

The boy handed her a charcoal sketch, and she sat down on the step to look at it. She was proud of this brother of hers, whose drawing more than once had caused the townsfolk to open their eyes wide. Almost a year before the schoolmaster declared he had talent and might become a painter some day, and since then he had improved much. Her eyes brightened with pleasure as she studied this sketch, for to her it seemed the finest he had ever made. It was a small drawing, no larger than her two brown hands, but it represented a company of angels scattering flowers and fruit in the path of Veronica Gambara, and every figure was perfectly proportioned and clear. She asked that she might keep it to show to some of her friends, tucked it into her bodice, and together they went to the plaza to join the revelers, where there was to be a feast for the townsfolk provided by Ghiberto in honor of his bride.

Then, gay indeed was the evening! Bonfires were lighted and torches gleamed through the olive trees, turning the artichokes and lentils in the garden patches into fantastic creatures, and dancing feet sped to low, delicious music as accordions swelled and shrank between sensitive, skilful fingers. Now some merry masker broke through the crowd and offered a nosegay to whoever could guess his identity, now a husky village youth gave an exhibition of physical skill, Antonio with the rest. At midnight the festivities ended in a blaze of artificial light, and the people went to their homes to remember the glad holiday through many a year to come, to give to their children and their children's children the story of the time when Veronica came among them as a bride. But little did they know that day was the beginning of something that will be a glory to Correggio as long as the world lasts.

Now it happened that Catarina had a friend who was a sister to one of the guards at the palace. To her she showed the drawing, and the girl, thinking it quite wonderful, took it to the soldier brother, who called his captain's attention to it, and finally it came under the notice of Veronica herself. It pleased the Princess to be portrayed so delightfully, and amazed her to know it was done by a fourteen-year-old. Like most of the great folk of Italy of that day, she understood art and recognized talent when she found it, and that very afternoon the baker's boy was summoned into her presence.

He was putting loaves into the stone oven when the messenger came with the word, and his ruddy face was redder still from the heat. Upon hearing that the Princess wanted to see him, he believed there must be some mistake, and after he got to the palace wished very much he had not gone. Being short and stocky and rather clumsy, he was much abashed in the presence of the royal lady. He was at home in his father's whitewashed cottage and in the garden patch in the shadow of the artichokes, where he bent over his paper and charcoal through many a summer afternoon, and there he knew just what to do with his hands and feet. But in the palace of Correggio they were woefully in the way, and he wished his peasant costume contained ruffles or pockets or something where he could hide them. But when Veronica Gambara began to talk of pictures, his awkwardness fled. He forgot that he was a baker's son who did not know court ways, and his eyes gleamed as they had gleamed that day when the royal coach went by.

The Lady of Correggio told him of the work of Andrea de Mantegna, a most illustrious artist of Mantua, and of Master Leonardo da Vinci, who was then doing wonderful things in Milan, not far away, and as he listened fascinated, exclaimed, "It is my dream to become a painter!"

Then Veronica smiled that rare smile of

hers that had inspired poets to write sonnets and caused men to call her, "The flower of the house of Pio," and answered in a low voice, "I shall help to make that dream come true."

She kept her word. From that day the Lady of Correggio was the friend and patron of the baker boy, and from that day Antonio sketched and painted as he never had done before. He worked with a mighty purpose, for now that Veronica chose to aid him, he knew his father would not stand in his way and insist that he become a tradesman, as once he had wished him to do. Almost nothing is known of his teachers. His uncle gave him some instruction, but his talent was so great that, almost unguided, it expressed itself in work such as Correggio had never seen.

Then, when seventeen, something happened that proved a blessing in disguise to Antonio Allegri. The plague broke out in his home town, and the royal family and many of the people fled to Mantua for safety. The young artist went with the rest, and there, for the first time in his life, beheld the work of a master painter. He began studying the pictures of Mantegna and learned much that he applied to his own work. Returning to Correggio some months later he toiled steadfastly, and day by day Veronica, who delighted in his improvement, marveled at his progress. Now she was very sure he would become a successful painter, but she did not dream that four centuries after her time people from all over the world would go to the town as to a shrine, not to see the palace where the lords of the land had lived, but to behold the spot where Antonio the baker's boy first stretched his canvases, and where he lived and worked and died. Yet that very thing came to pass.

Strange events sometimes shape the careers of men, and a strange and picturesque one now helped to shape that of Antonio Allegri. In Parma, forty miles away, was the Convent of San Paolo, one of the richest institutions of Italy. Its abbess was Donna Giovanna Piacenza, daughter of a powerful nobleman, and every nun within its walls was from one of the lordly houses of Italy. These women loved beautiful things and could afford to have them around them. The pavements over which they walked were adorned with exquisite tile work, and every year or two some artist was employed to brighten the walls and ceilings with frescoes. One day Abbess Giovanna made up her mind to have a chamber decorated, and hearing from her friend Veronica Gambara of the excellent work of the young painter of Correggio, decided to employ him. So word came to Antonio that he should go to Parma, and he left the low stone house among the artichokes and started on the way, walking all the distance and carrying his painter's supplies with him.

Those he passed thought him a clumsy country peddler bound for the next village to sell his wares, and when the Abbess Giovanna saw how like a simple peasant he looked, she feared she had made a mistake in entrusting the commission to this crude youth, and wished she had employed a finished artist. But great was her surprise when she beheld the completed chamber, and she exclaimed to her legal adviser, "All Italy will come to honor this favorite of Veronica!"

But Antonio did not hear her words of delight, for he was already on his way back to Correggio, hurrying along the dusty highway toward the whitewashed cottage, rejoicing in the satisfaction of work well done.

This was the beginning of great appointments for him. The beauty of the frescoes in the Convent of San Paolo soon became the talk of Parma, and other commissions were given to the young artist. So back to the city he went, first to paint in the Church of St. John the Evangelist, later in the Cathedral, and again his work amazed all who saw it, just as it had amazed the abbess and the nuns, just as it had amazed Veronica Gambara on that sunny April day. The pearl and gold of his flesh tints, the white and orange and rose of his draperies, were unsurpassed even by the master painters of Italy. Neither Raphael nor Titian of Cadore had produced more exquisite work, and his fame traveled. Orders came to him from princes and nobles, but while he executed them with wonderful success, they did not spoil him. He was a man of simple tastes and went on in the old, simple way. Still he lived and worked in the quiet of his home town, surrounded by his children and those of his sister Catarina, and only a few times in his life did he leave it. Up in the splendid city of Mantua dwelt the brilliant and beautiful Isabella d'Este, a princess powerful as she was fair. She was the friend of Veronica Gambara, and several times Antonio went to her court. But he was not at home there. He could work better in the peace of Correggio among the peasant folk he had known from childhood, and there he stayed.

At that time Italy was in the full glory of the Renaissance, and not far away were cities where marvelous things were being done, but the baker's son did not visit them. He never saw the Venice of Titian and Tintoretto, the Florence where Giotto and Michael Angelo and Andrea del Sarto wrought their wizardry, the imperial city beside the yellow Tiber where Raphael toiled and achieved. His genius was so great he did not need to seek

WHEN THE PRINCESS PASSED 253

inspiration in the creations of other men, but found it in the skies of morning and evening, the glory of the sun at midday, and in the deep blue silence of the starry night. Instead of gazing across the lagoons that gladdened the eyes of the Venetian painters, he looked out over a sea of vines where vintagers danced when the harvest was over, where scarlet and purple and orange headshawls of peasant women, bending to their work in the sun, gave him ideas of color. Instead of going far to seek models, the eyes and cheeks and lips of the village girls became his pictured faces, while his cherubs and angels were the laughing children who played in the streets of his native town. Perhaps sometimes he dreamed of journeying to the Milan of Leonardo da Vinci. Perhaps he had visions of some day seeing Rome with its Vatican and Borghese Villa—perhaps, but we do not know. We know only that he stayed on in Correggio, and that at forty years of age he died there, in the cottage with its trellis of climbing roses where for so many years he had lived and worked.

Then, as time passed, people grew to appreciate more and more the genius of Antonio Allegri, and canvases for which he had received very small sums became priceless. Every lord of the land wanted to possess something by Correggio, for, as was the custom in those days, they called him by the name of his native town. Powerful nobles tried to buy his work from churches and convents that held it, and sometimes, being not for sale, carried it away by force. This happened to "The Holy Night," one of his masterpieces now in the gallery of Dresden. The Duke of Modena tried to obtain it by fair means, and, failing in his aim, seized it by foul, leaving the little town in mourning when he robbed it of its treasure. This glorious painting passed from one lordly house to another, until finally, becoming the property of Augustus of Saxony, it came to be one of the art gems of Germany.

"The Madonna of St. Jerome," generally called "The Day," has a similar story. For many years it remained in the church for which it was painted, until the people, fearing for its safety, placed it in the Cathedral of Parma under guard. But that guard meant

WHEN THE PRINCESS PASSED 255

nothing to Napoleon Bonaparte, who came with his army and took it, carrying it off to France. But after many years and through much effort, Italy got it back, and to-day it beautifies the *duomo* (cathedral) from which it was stolen, the very one in which, long before, Antonio set his scaffolding and painted frescoes.

Many galleries in many different lands now glory in the work of Correggio. It is scattered throughout Europe, in Austria-Hungary, Germany, England, France, Spain, and Russia, as well as over Italy, which seems strange indeed when one stops to think that he who painted these pictures was never more than forty miles away from his native town. But in no one place in the world is as much of it to be found as in Parma. The Convent of San Paolo, the municipal gallery, the Church of St. John the Evangelist, and the duomo are all rich in his creations. There they are to be beheld on canvas and in fresco form, all marvelously beautiful, all flooded with that peculiar gold and pearly light, the secret of which was known to this master only. In this one city his work is to be seen in such glorious array that Ludwig Tieck, the German poet and critic, once exclaimed in wonderment, "Let no one think he has seen Italy, let no one believe he has learned the lofty secrets of art, until he has seen thee and thy cathedral, O Parma!"

By which he means the work of Antonio Allegri, better known as Correggio, the baker boy, who stood with the gleaming eyes of one who has beheld a vision when Princess Veronica Gambara, the flower of the house of Pio, passed on her way to the palace to become the bride of the young Lord Ghiberto.

THE JOYOUS VAGABOND

XIV

THE JOYOUS VAGABOND

THE boy sprang to his feet and leaned forward, listening. Could it be as late as that? It seemed not more than ten minutes he had dreamed there on the edge of the grotto, and now the cathedral bells were ringing, and he remembered that at home they would be saying the Angelus. He bent his head and clasped his hands, murmuring the words his mother had taught him back there in the fields of Lorraine, when the ocher of gloaming was on the pastures and chimes sounded out, calling across the hamlets from the dome of Nancy. Then, picking up his cap and birch staff, he started home, following the goat trail to the town.

Briskly, sturdily he swung on his way, as if to make up for lingering so long. Then suddenly he stopped and stood still. Some one was coming down the road that led from the French frontier.

His big eyes grew bigger as he looked, as if doubting, wondering. Could he be mistaken? Then a flush of pleasure overspread his face and he gave a joyous cry.

"Uncle Pierre," he called, "oh, Uncle Pierre!" and ran toward the advancing pedestrians.

There were three of them, men in caps and garments not of the Baden country, and they were dust stained and travel worn. The foremost of the group, taller and more sturdily built than the others, smiled like one who has suddenly heard good news.

"Well, to be sure," he exclaimed blithely, " 'tis my own sister's lad, Claude Gellee."

And then two brown hands were clasped in greeting.

Eastward, below the purple line of fir and spruce that marked the beginning of the Black Forest Mountains, the Rhine moved like a jeweled serpent in the sunset, and beyond, as if guarding the treasure, stood Säntis, opal-tinted. There was no fairer sight in all Germany, and a gipsy love of the open

THE JOYOUS VAGABOND 261

was in the boy's heart. It was for a glimpse of this rare view he had left his brother's shop in Freiburg and trudged three miles across the uplands after a hard day's work. It was the lure of sheeny river and fantastic peak, melting amethyst, coral, and smoke gray into violet stretches of sky line, that had held him there until sunset time, forgetful of the fact that there were chores to do at home and that he owed much, very much, to his brother. But now he seemed not to see. He talked eagerly and rapidly, asking for bits of news and gossip from beyond the mountains. Were the roses in the curé's garden as red as ever this summer, and did old Mère le Brun still suffer from rheumatism? It was good to hear from the distant village, and the sound of the French tongue was sweet to his ears. For Claude was not a German lad, nor had his childhood days been passed in Freiburg.

Westward, in that green and gold valley where the Moselle swings in gleaming festoons to meet the Rhine, the cottage of his fathers stood on the plains of Nancy. There he had lived, a merry peasant lad, until the year before when his parents died and the village was no longer home. He was just twelve years old, but hereafter must make his own way in the world, and realizing this, he thought of a calling more to his liking than that of a toiler in the fields. So he crossed the mountains to Freiburg, where his brother was established as a wood-carver.

"Is n't he a spry stripling to have come alone and on foot all the way from Lorraine?" the uncle asked his companions as he told the story. "Did n't beg his bread like a worthless lout, either," he continued with thrifty peasant pride, "but earned it by honest labor along the way. And now Jean writes he has made much progress at wood-carving. Do you like the craft, lad?"

Claude nodded, setting his Black Forest cap farther back on his head as he spoke.

"Yes, it is fun to see the figures grow out of the blocks."

And he gave a glowing description of life in Freiburg and home with his brother.

They were near the town now, so near that the Gothic spire of the Munster seemed directly overhead, and half way up a narrow

THE JOYOUS VAGABOND 263

side street he could see Jean driving the geese before him. He was sorry about that, for it was his work to bring them from the herbage field, and he had not meant to stay away so late. But he would do without his ramble to-morrow and make up for to-day's tardiness by working until dark.

But if Jean felt any anger toward his belated brother he forgot it when he saw the familiar garments of Lorraine and heard the loved *patois* of his native valley. He led them into the building that was both shop and home, where they laughed and talked over the meal that was soon spread for them, telling all the news of the old village.

"We may stay here for three days and enjoy life in our good French fashion," the uncle announced as they talked of the joy of meeting. "Then we must on to Rome to sell our wares."

For they were lacemakers, who once each year made the trip to Italy to dispose of their handiwork, and had little time for anything save toil. But those three days were theirs for rest and pleasure, during which they might forget the world held any cares.

They told stories and bits of gossip, joking and singing in the merry peasant way until the Freiburgers who lived close by wondered why there was such high revelry in the house of Gellee the carver.

Next morning Claude was up at dawn. There were chickens to feed and geese to be driven to pasture, and he wanted to be through before the visitors awoke. Their time together would be short at best, and then a year would pass before they met again. So he meant to be with the uncle as much as possible.

The cathedral bells were chiming six when he came back and went into the shop to assort the tools. They would do less work than usual that day, because of hours to be given over to the guests. But there was an altar piece for the church at Rosenheim, an order that could not be delayed, and things must be made ready for Jean to finish it. He moved back and forth, putting knives and files and tracers where his brother could lay hands upon them, and while he worked his uncle came in.

"Jean says you have made much progress,"

THE JOYOUS VAGABOND 265

he said as he looked at the bits of carving, finished and unfinished, that were scattered about on the tables. "Have you done any of these?"

Claude went over to where he stood.

"Yes, some of them," he answered. "With the big ones I helped and this one I did alone."

And he designated a tray of silver larchwood, on which a flock of birds were skimming over tree tops.

The uncle examined it carefully, and as he looked nodded his head as if thinking. Claude wondered what was in his mind, but asked no questions.

"I hope he thinks I have done well," he thought as he watched him.

Then he heard his brother coming in from the garden.

The lacemaker looked up with a smile when he saw Jean standing in the doorway.

"Claude has been showing me his carving," he remarked, "and I've an idea about him."

The boy stood still, listening, waiting. Did he consider his work good or bad? He had put his best effort into it, and the brother had often praised the result. Would his uncle praise it, too?

Then came a glad surprise.

"He has done marvelously well," the lace-maker said, as he held up the beautiful bit of handiwork. "It seems he has a gift for carving, and methinks there is more in store for him than being a wood-worker."

And he told stories he had heard in Rome, of youths from far provinces who had gone there penniless and unknown, but being possessed of genius had grown to be glorious artists and men of great estate. Might not Claude, his own sister's lad, be one of that number? And before the boy realized what it was all about, they decided that he should go to Rome.

Rome! The word had a magical sound to his ears. It was far from Freiburg, he knew, across mountains and plains, many leagues farther than his native Lorraine, that seemed so distant. He would see gleaming palaces and great nobles and splendid statues and pictures, hundreds of them, done by masters of chisels and colors. In

THE JOYOUS VAGABOND 267

those days there were no railroads connecting the North and the South, and the lacemakers, being poor, would take the journey on foot, selling their wares and earning board and lodging as they went. Leagues of highland, leagues of lowland, and perhaps trails drifted over with snow. But what of that? Beyond was a city of unnumbered splendors, which might seem fairer and more incomparable after days and nights of vagabonding.

So southward through the Black Forest they journeyed, wood-carver's apprentice and lacemakers three, toward the land where there would be money in exchange for wares, and perhaps glory undreamed of for Claude. Across Switzerland they went, and through the Italian Alps, past lake and fell, into pink and gold Tuscany. Florence, Lily of the Arno, with her matchless gardens and palaced boulevards, was alluring then as she is to-day, but Florence was not their destination. Resting there a few days, in a house overlooking the river, Claude helped to dispose of some of the laces. Then they moved down the valley toward Rome.

Were his dreams of the glories of the place realized? Ah yes! It seemed a magic land in which he dwelt, where all the streets were enchanted gardens and all the people folk of Elfland, and when he went to the great buildings that housed the works of art he wondered how so many noble ones came to be in the world. Day after day he dreamed among them, thinking of nothing save their beauty and color, planning for nothing but that some day he, too, should join the company of creators.

Then something unexpected happened, causing the uncle to leave Rome immediately. That meant one of two things for Claude. He must return to the North or stay in a city whose language he could neither speak nor understand, with little money in his pocket and small prospect of getting any from his relatives. But he didn't study long. He looked at the pictures that had opened wonderland to him, and when his uncle put the question he answered, "I stay."

So with five sous in his pocket and a mighty hope in his heart, Claude Gellee began life as a solitary lad in Rome. In a poor quarter near the Tiber he found cheap lodgings, spending hours every day in the studios and galleries among the treasures to be seen there. Sometimes he ground colors for a painter, sometimes turned choreboy, making enough to supply his modest wants, and sometimes—he went hungry. But did his courage fail him, did he think of returning north? Not once. He might have gone back to Freiburg to the workshop of his brother, or to Lorraine where his uncle lived, and gleaned and sowed in the fields. But no! He had come to Rome to try his fortune, to be an artist if God willed it, and in Rome he meant to stay. Once in a while a little money came from the carver brother in Germany, once in a while; but the sums were small and the times far, far apart. Then the Thirty Years' War broke out and Jean could send nothing more. So Claude was thrown solely on his own efforts, the very greatest of which did not suffice to pay for bed and board and the teaching he craved. But he would not give up. He stayed on and on, studying the treasures, working without instruction, making use of the simple art principles taught him by his brother, trying to help himself by watching and doing. On velvet summer nights when pleasure-loving Romans thronged the *vias* he lay on a clump of weeds beyond the city wall, watching the play of moonlight on the Alban hills; while in the perfumed dawning, when the pulse of the city was still in sleep, he was up before birds called and out on the Campagna, to see the rose and gold of sunrise gleam out of the gray, to mark the line of shadow along the copsewood, and note the position of the sun at every change. Too poor to afford teachers, he went to Nature, master of them all, believing always, hoping always, that some day he would become an artist.

One morning, as he roamed back and forth, looking at canvases in one of the great treasure houses, he came upon a painting by Goffreddo. It was a landscape with broad reaches of sea and wooded shore, and dim, fantastic in the misty background, palaces with domes and spires; blue in the sky, saffron and mauve on the sea, and a silver haze, like a wind-blown gossamer floating along the tree tops. Nothing seen in Rome had delighted him so, and as he looked and looked again he thought, "That is how I want to paint. I will find Goffreddo and see if he will teach me."

Successful artists in that day were acclaimed throughout Italy, and although living in a distant city the abiding place was well known. So it was with Goffreddo. Almost the first person Claude asked told him where to find the master.

"He is in Naples," said a rich patron of one of the studios he frequented, wondering why a shabbily clad peasant lad should care to know.

Claude knew the location of Naples. It was to the southward, a good hundred and fifty miles. But what of that? Distance, lack of traveling funds, could be no check to one who had gone companionless and on foot from the fields of Lorraine to the hills of Freiburg, and again on foot, by Swiss lakes and Italian plains to the Eternal City. He would go to Naples, to Naples where the master dwelt, and since there was no money to pay his fare by chaise, what would serve him better than his sturdy peasant legs? So to Naples he went, earning his bread *en route* as he had earned it two years before crossing the Vosges Mountains, and in Naples he found Goffreddo.

"Better seek some labor here and make enough to get back to Rome," a loiterer in the street said in answer to his question when he asked the way to the studio of the painter. "Goffreddo will not receive you, for he is selfish and hard, or if he does he will make your life so miserable you'll rue the day you met him. Believe me, he is a merciless task-master."

But Claude would not heed his words. Had he gone hungry in Rome and taken the long journey through a bandit-infested country only to give up the thing of his dreams when it seemed within his reach? He wanted to be a painter, and Goffreddo was the master he meant to have. So, undaunted by discouraging advice, he sought the artist's door.

Perhaps it was the story of his days and nights of hardship, perhaps the light in the glowing eyes that bespoke the dreamer's soul, but something touched the master who was

Wonderful roseate days began

THE JOYOUS VAGABOND 275

called severe and unhelpful, something made him feel that Claude deserved a trial. He received him into his studio, and wonderful, roseate days began.

Life in Naples was much as it had been in Rome. He ground Goffreddo's colors and kept the workshop in order, earning his food about the city by doing various kinds of labor. And what a dream city it was, with a glittering sky above a glittering bay and miles and miles of rainbow-colored terraces! He loved to watch Vesuvius, standing there like a giant wrapped in mist, loved to see the fisher boats float like fairy liners from far seaward, the swarthy rowers singing as they neared the wharf of Santa Lucia. And often, when there was a little time to spare, he pictured some of the scenes in the street: the children, bare of head and bare of feet, the goats that browsed along the *vias,* and the girls and women who laughed at him from under scarlet kerchiefs. But most of all he delighted in painting the weird, dark cypress trees, the groves of plane and oleander encompassing some princely residence, the stretches of rainbow-colored reef out

Sorrento way, and the gleam of rose and purple Capri in the afterglow. The hours other boys would have spent in play he passed with pencils, drawing-board and colors. And when Goffreddo saw how well he did he smiled and nodded his head.

"Yes, Claude," he spoke one day as he watched him work, "it was meant for you to be a landscape painter."

And the boy, rejoicing, painted more feverishly than before.

Two years passed in the city of Vesuvius, with rambles along the iridescent bay and never-to-be-forgotten hours in the studio of the master. Then Goffreddo being unable to keep him longer, he returned to Rome as he had come to Naples, vagabonding, and took up his work more earnestly than ever. Agostino Tassi was his teacher, and again he paid for his lessons by color grinding and turning choreboy, watching, listening, laboring, improving every hour, until his work grew so excellent that orders came in for his pictures, and he opened a studio of his own.

From that time forth fortune smiled on Claude. He painted tirelessly, unceasingly, always on the landscapes he loved so much, and always his creations found a ready market. Then word of the beauty of his canvases reached Pope Urban, who commissioned him to make four pictures for the Papal Palace, which were so exquisitely done that one art lover exclaimed, "Such glorious work must be that of angels," and he had more orders than he could fill. His landscapes were in such demand and brought such high prices that only the very rich could afford to own them, and he came to be what his uncle, the lowly lacemaker, had dreamed he might become, a glorious artist and a man of great estate.

And still he stayed on in Rome, among the scenes where he had grown to success, painting the sublime sunsets of the Campagna, the quiet peaceful bays and coves of Naples that had left an indelible impress on his heart, and loving France with an exile's love. Once he went back, spending a year in the haunts of his childhood, but the scenes he pictured most wonderfully were those of the Italian land, so to Rome he returned, never again to leave it.

But always he remembered that he was a Frenchman. He never forgot that his cradle rocked in Lorraine, never ceased to love the valley where he had lived, a peasant boy. And because of the place of his nativity and his great love for it, they gave him his country's name, and he who was born Claude Gellee is known to fame as Claude Lorraine. For undying fame he won. Guileless toiler from the banks of the Moselle, joyous, dreaming vagabond, he grew to be the king of landscape painters, the brightest star in the art of France. The beauty of his canvases is incomparable, and although gifted, ambitious men have been striving to equal him for over two hundred years, no one has succeeded. Still he stands alone, the master portrayer of nature, of whom Sir Joshua Reynolds said, "We may sooner expect to see another Raphael than another Claude Lorraine."

Is it therefore strange that France is proud to have her immortal son bear the name of one of her great provinces?